The Whites Next Door

and other erotic tales

by Jay Cuze

36,760 words

ISBN 978-0-9841603-3-4

A Word from Jay

Hard to believe that at one time I was as active and as randy as the next man. Now, I'm forced to spend pretty much all of my time confined to a wheel chair.

My Cadillac is equipped with hand controls, and I have a portable folding chair that will fit in the trunk, but as I still need someone to help me in and out of my car, it stays in the garage most of the time.

Being confined in my home this way doesn't mean that I'm blind or deaf. Move aside a curtain and I can see up and down the block of single-family homes, nice homes at that. Thank God, the nearest apartments—rabbit hutches I call them, are several blocks away.

This block has some good-looking women. (Another good thing about being as old as I am, whether they're 16 or sixty, the girls look awfully good to me.)

I've Linda on one side of me, Adriana on the other. Both have husbands, though it doesn't seem to bother them any. When I was still driving, every so often I'd come across Adriana's car parked where it oughtn't to be. She's a mature woman, too, with two teenagers, a girl and a boy. You'd think she'd have settled down by now. (By the way, like me, Adriana doesn't seem to have any age barriers.)

Linda is considerably younger, all fresh faced and innocent, with breasts the size of cannon balls. She's been kind enough to oblige me on several occasions, sitting in my lap and letting me bury my face between them.

More often, I take my satisfaction with Liz, another married woman, who lives over in the apartments. She's married, also, and was very devoted to her husband until it happened. Guess I ought to tell you about her, too.

Joanne lives across the street. She's lived there almost as long as I have. Saw her and her husband raise a child, a girl, not quite so pretty as Joanne. One moment, she's in Bluebirds, then Guides. The next, their daughter is in college, and the last I see of her is the day they set up a canopy across the street and held her wedding reception.

Joanne adapts to her empty nest after a few months and gets a job as a realtor. Does real good at it, too. Then her husband up and dies. Poor woman is distraught, mopes about the house all day. I'm thinking maybe I should pay her a visit, wheel me across the street. But the new neighbors beat me to it.

Think I'll tell Joanne's story first. She had the farthest to fall, so her story is a long one. It all began as so many of these affairs do with the first African Americans to move onto our block.

The Whites Next Door

Prolog

"Well, has he or hasn't he?"

"He's just 15."

"15! I was 14! What's the matter with him, is he gay."

"I doubt that." Marge White folded her arms across her more than ample chest.

"You doubt that he's gay?"

"I doubt you were 14. Eighteen, maybe. I've seen the pictures of the young Norman. Besides, Noble is shy."

"Shyness is no excuse. He's got to meet girls. He does like girls?"

"Of course, he likes girls. Have you seen his photo collection?"

Mr. White had seen his fifteen year old's collection, part of which he had donated to the boy to point him in the right direction.

"I don't mean the photos you gave him," Marge continued as if she'd read her husband's mind, "I mean the ones he took himself of our neighbor."

"Miss Nose in the air?"

"Mrs., she's a widow. And she really is very friendly. If you'd give her a chance."

"Skinny white lady, nose in the air, I don't think so."

"Ah, but do you think she is good enough for our son?"

New Neighbors

The new family next door, the Whites, really didn't fit into the neighborhood.

It bothered Jo that she should feel this way about them. For apart from their color—the Whites were black—they fit the neighborhood quite well. Perhaps, for their five-bedroom house was large, their cars expensive, they would have made an even better fit in a more upscale location—a Bel Air rather than a Brentwood, a Flintridge rather than a La Canada, an Anaheim Hills rather than an Anaheim.

Not that she had any aspirations of her own to move farther up the ladder. Her house was perfect—thank you very much—it sat on a third-of-an acre lot—and now that her husband was gone and her daughter away at college, it was just a bit more than she could handle.

Mr. White—she did not yet know his first name—drove a huge Lincoln—a realtor's car, and Jo surmised that he owned his own business. He was often away for days at a time and whenever his car turned up in his driveway, he would be on the cell phone in a conversation that often went on long after he was parked.

Marge White drove a sporty two-seater Mercedes. The car looked small on her, for she was a big woman, broad tipped, and ample bosomed. "I's a big woman all over," she said once in a put-on ghetto accent for she normally spoke perfect English.

The Whites had their groceries delivered mostly while Jo always went to the store herself. She'd done so even when her husband was alive, and now, of course, she couldn't afford to do anything else.

Jo loved her own house with its backyard pool, though the daily cleaning the pool required could be a chore. The Whites had both a terraced outdoor pool and indoors, a swim-in-place. She could occasionally glimpse shadowy figures through the frosted glass.

The Whites had a 17 or 18-year-old son named Noble who went to the local high school. At least, she supposed he did. The boy didn't seem to have made any friends yet, so she couldn't be sure whether he was in high school or junior college.

There was a second son, also, much older, who put in the occasional rare appearance, usually in a full-dress army uniform.

He could have been Mrs. White's brother, of course, rather than her son. Jo really didn't have any way of knowing. In fact, given the number of months the Whites had lived next door to her, it was amazing how little she knew about them.

This bothered her. She knew all her other neighbors, but not the Whites. She wasn't a racist; she knew that. She'd gone to school with Hispanics and although she hadn't actually dated any of them, they'd been friends.

No, her not knowing them was simply another part of the grief process, her almost-complete withdrawal from society after her husband's death. This was a pity, for she was still a relatively young woman albeit one with a college-age daughter, and her body still firm and desirable was simply going to waste.

The time came—it was inevitable that it would—when she and Mrs. White pulled into their driveways one morning at almost the same moment. When Jo got out of the car to carry her groceries in the house, there was Mrs. White to give her a hand. And from then on it was Marge and Jo.

Making Friends

The Whites had not been well-to-do long, Marge confided. But they had been moving steadily upward during the past decade. "It's the Internet. Joe doesn't understand how it works or even how to hook up our own computer, but he's really made it pay off for us."

Jo wasn't sure just how the Internet had paid off for the Whites or what it was they sold exactly. But she knew it had made Marge very happy. The White's house was the proof. "Each of our houses has been bigger and better. And the neighborhoods. This is such a wonderful place to live. And the schools are excellent."

Thus it was that Jo learned the names of the White's two sons, Noble the youngest who lived at home and was just about to finish high school, and Roland who had graduated two years earlier and was in the Marines. "I would have liked to delay the move until Nobel had graduated—he would at least have had a few friends, but we'd no choice but to move now." Marge told her.

Jo also had started to meet Marge's friends, most of who were left over from the previous neighborhoods in which the Whites had lived. An older friend Millie, a cousin of Marge's, was a frequent visitor to Marge's along with two of her friends whose names Jo learned and as quickly forgot. Another regular caller was Velma, a younger woman, with a truly startling bosom, "False," Marge confided, "She gets them bigger every year."

Marge was quick to confide in Jo although Jo was not sure she wanted to hear all that Marge had to relate. Millie was post-menopausal, had hot flashes, and a husband who was demanding as ever. Marge's own husband had moods; he was also, Marge suggested, uncaring, "he wants oral sex and forgets about me." But, "he was a very good provider," and Jo gathered that in Marge's view this was what really counted. "Besides," Marge's said with put-on accent, "They's plenty of younger mens who likes big titties" and shook her giant bosoms by way of illustration.

To Jo's relief, Marge did not demand equal confidences in return. Jo did not want to discuss her own sex life, which had been virtually non-existent since her husband's death.

In truth, it had been non-existent unless one counted the deputy sheriff who had informed her of her husband's accident. He'd come back later, held Jo in his arms, stroked her hair, played with her bosoms, and although she'd had an orgasm as they stood for what had seemed an hour in her living-room, pressed against each other, at the last moment she'd asked him to leave. Since then, nothing.

"She needs to be milked," Jo had overheard Millie say of her. And it was probably true. Jo missed the loving attention her late husband had given to each of her small breasts.

A Game of Whist

Marge swam in Jo's pool. And Jo swam in Marge's.

Occasionally, Marge would swim nude in the indoor pool, not when the children were there of course, but Jo couldn't quite bring herself to do it.

"What if your son comes home?"

"Oh poo, look at the clock."

Marge had a beautiful body, not fat as Jo had first surmised but big-boned, ample, with all the bosom a man could ask for and perhaps a tad more. And hips, Marge said, broad enough to guarantee a man would not fall off. Jo couldn't recall a man ever falling off her own and giggled.

In the afternoons, Marge would often have friends over to play whist. At first, Jo, who had absolutely no idea what the game was about, would just watch. Then she was persuaded to play a few hands, "at least until Millie shows up."

And then, abruptly, she was a regular at the table, and both the cards and money in front of her were hers.

Innocent and innocuous though the penny per point game of whist seemed, somehow, one afternoon, Jo had lost two hundred dollars.

"Don't worry," Marge assured her. "I took care of it."

"But you can't," Jo stammered, "Two hundred dollars. That's too much. I'll pay you back."

"Don't be silly. You don't owe me anything. Besides, I got you into the game. Anyway, the money didn't come out of my pocket. I simply explained to everyone that this was your first time and it would be unfair to take advantage of you."

Relief swept through her. "It was my first time. Well, the first time I lost that much money."

Marge laughed. "You do owe me a favor, though."

"Anything," Jo said. She was immensely grateful, pleased a debt she could not afford had been so easily swept away.

"I want you to go out with my son."

"Marshall?" Jo thought that was the name of the son that served in the army.

"No, Noble. Now don't give me that strange look. He's at the age where he should be dating girls, but he's too shy, and he doesn't know anyone who might just fix him up with a blind date. There are girls in his class, girls all around the school. But he doesn't know how to ask them, and when I tell him how easy it is, he'll say, 'Where shall I take them and what if I don't do the right thing?'

"You know how it is, you had teenagers."

"A girl," said Jo, "But I do understand."

"I want him to take you to a movie."

"But why me? I mean surely one of your friends." Jo realized she'd almost said, one of your African-American friends, and blushed.

"You mean one of my colored friends? Don't apologize." She added when Jo continued blushing. "There's something you should know and that's the reason I chose you.

"Follow me." Marge led the way down a long hallway to her son's room. It was everything to be expected of a teenager's bedroom though perhaps neater than most. A desk, a rug, a bed. A poster of Puff Daddy on the door and one of Kobe Bryant above the desk. A closet whose door closed and locked, Jo hoped, so the boy could at least have some area that could be considered private.

A bureau held a series of trophies. Noble must be some kind of athlete. One for Little League, one for soccer, but most were for basketball.

Photos were also taped to the wall about the bed, candid snaps rather than the staged photographs on the wall above the bureau. "Take a look at these," Marge said with a wave of her hand.

Each and every photograph was of Jo, snipping roses, collecting mail, or simply walking into her house grocery bags in hand.

Most of the snapshots were in side view revealing a bust that Jo had never realized she possessed. Her breasts filled a B-cup at best, had filled out to a C only once late in her last pregnancy. Not more than a mouthful.

Marsha saw where Jo was looking. "I loved breast feeding," she said, "I hope you did too.

"Noble and Marshall were both rabid feeders. My husband does his best, but it's not quite the same. I'm always having to shout, 'Suck harder.'"

Jo blushed, remembering. She still couldn't believe how casual Marsha and her black friends were about sex. Sexual references and stories had occupied most of the conversation at the whist table.

Breast-feeding was wonderful. And it had been a long time, even since her husband had. If the truth were to be told and Jo certainly wasn't about to tell Marge, the first time she'd ever had an orgasm was while someone was fondling her breasts.

"You're blushing," Marge said. "Us black folk blush, too, it just doesn't show up as easy."

They both laughed at this and until Marge gave her a call almost a week later, she'd almost forgotten about her promise to go out with Marge's son.

First Date

"That dress won't do," Marge said and Jo was somewhat offended.

Jo thought the clothes she'd selected for the finally to-be-realized date with Noble were ideal. The baggy dark black ribbed sweater that fell to just below the hips of a stylish gray long skirt was both conservative as befit an older woman and flattering to her figure as befit a female who was really not all that old.

As Marge led Jo into what Marge called her sewing room, she said, "I want my son to think of you as a woman not a mother."

"Too conservative?"

"Exactly."

Marge reached into a pile of folded clothes and pulled out a gray cardigan. "Try this on instead," she said.

"It looks even more … "

"Try it on."

Jo changed clothes, feeling uneasy, as the cardigan was a good deal smaller and tighter than she felt comfortable with.

"It's the bra," Marge said. "Look in the mirror."

Marge was right. The cross-your-heart brassiere that had gone well with the baggy sweater had stretched the cardigan out of proportion. "Slip it off," Marge said, "I'll get you another one.

"No, don't take off the sweater, there isn't time." Jo wriggled like a contortionist slipping the bra off one shoulder and down the other and out a sleeve. Removing, then replacing the sweater, she thought would have been far less time consuming. Or had Marge simply wanted to watch her struggle.

An adolescent wail sounded from the hallway, and Marge slipped out of the room. "I'll kill him."

Apparently, Noble did not want to wear a jacket and was being told in no uncertain terms that he would wear the clothes his mother has laid out for him or else. This went a long way to explaining why Marge was so pushy; she was used to ordering men, a husband and two sons, around.

What Jo saw in the long vertical mirror opposite the sewing table while waiting for Marge to return was not at all reassuring. The sweater was the right length and its color went well with the gray of the skirt, but it was far too tight and without a bra was not much better than going topless.

"Time to go," Marge said almost the instant she re-entered the room. "Leave the boy alone for another minute and he'll either faint with fright or get his clothes dirty."

Jo couldn't believe Marge was serious about leaving. She was far from ready to go out. Where was the brassier Marge had gone to fetch? She gestured toward the mirror. Marge looked at the mirror, looked back at her, and then gave a shrug, "So?"

"My nipples are showing." And indeed Jo's nipples were standing upright like soldiers eager to leap forth from concealment.

"Oh pooh, you can handle it and him, too." was Marge's only comment. "He's going to learn to be a gentleman." And so braless, Jo went off with Noble on his (and her) first date.

Noble had said virtually nothing to her after a simple mumbled greeting in Marge's living-room so that she'd been forced to make most if not all of their initial conversation. He'd held the door open for her, but then, once outside the house, had started to run across the grass toward her car. An instant later, he'd stopped, as if suddenly remembering the instructions he'd received from his mother, and returned to walk sedately by Jo's side.

To her surprise, he waited by her car door till she was within, and only then dashed around to the passenger door. He was every inch a young pup who'd received one too many instructions. Not quite sure of all he'd learned, but desperate to please his mistress with what he did remember.

Jo wanted to laugh, but of course she couldn't, not without offending him. Instead, she gave what she hoped was a motherly smile.

Once underway, Noble quieted and again all efforts at conversation were left to Jo. His fingers reached out once for the radio, till remembering whose car it was and the instructions he'd been given, they dropped back frustrated in his lap.

"Would you like me to turn on the radio?"

"No mamm, no Mrs. Turner."

And it was no mamm and yes mamm to virtually all other questions including "do you like school?" and "what's your favorite sport?"

Occasionally, Noble would run a finger along his neck under his collar and tie—yes, he wore a tie—but for the most part he sat still, almost rigid.

When she glanced over at him occasionally, he would be staring straight ahead, though once, she was sure, he'd been staring sidelong at her. At the same view that was captured in his photographs, or because of the tight sweater she now wore, she realized blushing, a little more nipple showing.

The theater was a multiplex. This meant they had to go through a series of "what would you like to see?" "It doesn't matter, whatever you like." "No, you choose." In the end she'd named a picture she'd thought would please him. As it turned out, he wasn't sure that was the movie he'd bought tickets for or, later, if the movie for which he'd bought tickets was the one they actually saw.

He was very nervous. His only moment of take charge, one which reminded her curiously of his mother, was at the refreshment stand when without consulting her he bought two large 7-Ups—no problem, she liked 7-Up—and a large, no, a gigantic bucket of popcorn.

The bucket of popcorn, she could tell once they sat down, hid a marked erection.

He was so cute, yet so terrifying at the same time. What could one say to a boy that age that would put him at his ease? While they watched the previews, she thanked him for the popcorn, sipped her drink, and gave him several bright smiles.

Twice she caught him looking at her breasts, but that was to be expected, what with the tight sweater Marge had given her to wear and no bra.

Because he'd been so shy before, so inarticulate, the hand that reached up in the darkness after the lights went down in the theatre and touched her chest was all the more surprising.

Of course, she was partly to blame. She'd followed Marsha's instructions to some extent, letting her breast "accidentally" come in contact with his arm, taking his hand and touching his knee each time there was an exchange of popcorn. But still the hand on her breast was unexpected.

Even more unexpected were the fingers that had grasped and begun to stroke her right nipple. She ought to tell him to stop but the sensation was so pleasurable, the strokes and tugs were so gentle that she simply gave way to it.

What was showing on the screen was a blur. She looked up and down and to the side, but when once she looked at him, he was staring back with such intensity that she had to look away.

At some point, the hand had gone beneath the sweater and had begun to explore each breast in turn. His other hand had ventured once onto her thigh, but she'd grabbed his wrist before his hand could go further, had gripped it tightly while she had the first of her orgasms and heard him give a cry of pain.

She'd had one and perhaps several orgasms by the time the lights went up and the film was over. I hope nobody asks me what the film was about, she thought inanely, because I don't remember anything.

What do you say to someone who is fifteen or sixteen who has taken you on a first date and given you more pleasure than you'd had in a almost a year, more pleasure then you ought to have let him give you on a seventh or eighth date? "Are you fifteen or sixteen?" she asked.

"Fifteen last week," he said.

"I ought to have given you a present."

Then they were walking up the aisle, across the lobby and into the fresh air. "It was a great picture," he said, "I liked it a lot." As if remembering yet another instruction he'd been given, he added, "Thank you for coming with me."

They sat quietly in the car for a few moments, till she remembered she needed to reach down and turn the key. She was driving after all. Before she could complete the action, he leaned toward her across the seat as if to kiss her. Quickly, she leaned away. Kissing wouldn't do at all, would only present the wrong message. But her lips had never been his intention. And retreating so that her head was back against the car door had only placed the real targets more firmly in his reach. It took only half a second for him to lift her sweater and his thick lips to engulf her turgid nipple.

The feeling was wonderful and it was all wrong. The sucking went on for several minutes though, five, then ten minutes, before it ceased momentarily.

Between, she'd resisted several attempts to have her place her hand in his lap but finally, worn down from the struggle she'd let her hand lie where he'd placed it.

His pants were damp; obviously, he'd already come once with excitement.

Her own crotch was damp and sticky. She wasn't sure how much more she could take of his form of lovemaking.

His sucking was so frenzied, just as his mother had described, that after awhile she asked him to wait. "My breast hurts," she said, and carefully transferred his attention to her other nipple. She held his head there for several moments, her hand gently cradling his neck.

"Finish me," he said.

She looked down at him puzzled. "I'm sorry," she said, "You'll have to stop; it's really beginning to hurt. Both of them. I'm out of practice."

"But I haven't come yet. I'm almost there." She could hear him unzipping but did not want to look down. She could imagine his penis though, big and black and throbbing. The next moment his big dick was in her hand and she was stroking it up and down as he'd requested.

It took only seconds before his cum filled her hand and began to drip from her arm. "Wait," he said and got out the handkerchief his mother had so obviously ironed and folded so he might look impressive on his date. He carefully dried her hand with the handkerchief, and then, unexpectedly, took the cum he'd gathered and held it to her lips. She tried to back away, but he separated her lips and poked the cloth inside. She licked the cum from the cloth as was his intention, then remained passive as he cleaned her arm and again brought the handkerchief to her mouth. Again she sucked the drops from the cloth.

"I've still got some 7-up left," he said. "Do you want it?"

She nodded and rinsed her mouth. "Why did you do that with the cloth?" she asked.

"My Dad told me girls really like it. Did you like it?"

She could tell he was eager to have her say that he did and would be disappointed if she were to say anything else. The fact was that she did like it and had missed the taste. She couldn't believe that at the same time, she was worrying about whether any had spilled on the sweater (which she would have to return—where had large-breasted Marge got such a small sweater from?) and how she wanted to take his penis in her mouth and suck the last few drops from its tip, though by now his penis was sure to be shriveled and small.

The parking lot grew dark suddenly as the lights of the movie theater were extinguished. She could see the last of the theater employees exiting the now-darkened theater.

"Are we goin' t'go?" he asked from the seat beside her. His voice was firm and controlled, no longer hesitant and unsure of itself.

She gave a half-ashamed smile and started the car. "I'll take you home." He reached over before tightening his safety belt and gave her a peck on the cheek. Something he must have seen his father do. And then they left the lot.

Rainy Day Afternoon

She had waited the next morning half-dreading and half-expecting Marge's call. But nine, and then ten, and then eleven a.m. came and went without Jo hearing from her.

The trip home in the darkness the night before had been relatively uneventful. She'd tried to drop Noble off in front of his house but he'd said, no, his mother had told him to see her home. She'd parked the car in her driveway, not wanting to be alone with him in her garage. He'd tried to put her hand on his penis anyway but she'd pulled away and his last failed attempt to grope her breast had been frustrated as she slipped out the driver's side of the car.

She hadn't frustrated much else he'd wanted that night. She hadn't gone entirely unfrustrated either and a flush spread over her body as she remembered how it had been in the car after the movie with his sucking first on her right nipple and then on the left.

She would not let it happen again. She could only hope he had not told his mother what had happened. At least, not everything.

What if Marge were to ask her how the date had gone?

She'd simply say that Noble had been very polite, had done all the things his mother had asked him to do, including, she wondered, feeling me up and later sucking on each of my nipples until they were sore. Had that been Marge's idea too? It was Marge after all who had insisted on her wearing that tight sweater, on removing her bra. Regardless, she was not about to tell her next-door neighbor and best friend that, "yes, your son was very polite and attentive and to thank him, I jerked him off and later licked and swallowed his cum."

But Marge did not call, had driven off, in fact, shortly after Noble had come home for lunch and had not yet returned when the skies opened a few hours later and began to dump rain in buckets on the streets.

When Noble showed up at Jo's door around four looking like a drenched rat and told her that he was locked out of the house, she didn't think twice before letting him in and escorting him into her living room. "Don't sit down, I'll get you a towel."

She got two towels, one that she gave him to dry his hair with and the other, which she put on her couch so he would have a place to sit. Since he seemed reluctant to use the first towel, some sort of man thing, she sat down on the couch beside him and set to work on his head with the towel herself.

It took only seconds and her sweater was pushed up, her bra as well, so that it had tightened against her chest and he was sucking passionately on her right nipple.

She had meant to say, "no, we're not going to do anything like this any more" but instead she was asking him to be gentle, telling him that her nipple still hurt from the previous night. He lifted his head then and slowly licked the nipple's tip instantly sending a flood of ecstasy through her entire body. Gratefully, she let him unsnap her brassiere, stroke the other nipple, then put her hand between his legs.

"No," she said, but he did not release her hand.

"Do you mind that I'm black?"

"No."

"Then why are you afraid to touch it."

"I'm not; you know I'm not. I just don't want to have you come on the couch. I need a cloth of some kind, a handkerchief."

He put the towel in her hand, then led her other hand down beneath where his testicles now swung free from his pants. She had barely wrapped her hands around the twin sacs, when he came in a great thrust, bathing the towel with his cum.

She was not surprised when a moment later he had begun to wipe her lips with the towel, waiting till she had sucked greedily at the drops, and then moving to a new portion of the cloth. He finished by reaching down to the tip of his penis, collecting the few remaining drops on his fingertips and rubbing his finger gently across her lips.

She wanted to hold him then and for a moment he let her.

The doorbell rang. He sprang to his feet. "No, sit down," she said, "Read a book or something." She retied her bra quickly, pulled down the sweater and smoothed her skirt. Then she went to answer the door.

As Jo had expected, the caller was Noble's mother. "Still together," Marge said with a wink, "I wondered when Noble didn't come home last night."

"Just joking." Marge said quickly and Jo wondered if her face had reddened, giving her away. "Noble, you've got to do your homework. Oh, you are doing it." She gestured toward the schoolbooks now open on the coffee table. "I'd just as soon you do your work at home and stop bothering our neighbor." Marge turned back then to Jo. "I shouldn't have left the house locked, but who knew it was going to rain and in buckets, too."

"No problem," Jo said. "He's no bother."

"There's a hen party tomorrow, can you come?"

Jo nodded and then, Marge had swept out the door pushing Noble ahead of her.

We pulled that off, Jo thought. Though she couldn't remember whether Noble pants had been zipped up and his belt buckled when she'd gone to answer the door. It was only when she looked in the mirror and spotted a near invisible spot of cum on her chin that she again wondered how successful their deception had been.

I pulled him off she thought, two days in a row. I swallowed the cum of a fifteen-year old. I can't do this again. I mustn't.

Two Morning Encounters

The next two days passed exactly as Jo had sworn they would and she was not sure she was happy this was the way things had turned out.

Noble had appeared once at her door after school and she had simply not answered it. The phone had rung several times that evening and she had let the answering machine take the call each time. There'd been heavy breathing and once she thought she'd heard the sounds Noble made just as he came, but the caller had not identified himself.

But she had plenty of work to do to fill her days. She'd only recently completed the real estate class and, while she'd yet to make a sale or complete a listing, she was no longer nervous in the presence of potential clients. Soon, she hoped, she'd begin to realize a steady income.

The third morning, Noble had appeared in her bedroom while she was still rubbing the sleep from her eyes.

She wasn't sure how he'd gotten in—surely all the doors were locked, but there he was.

He'd sat on the edge of her bed and immediately began playing with her breasts. She'd worn only a tank top to bed—the night was warm—and her nipples had literally no protection. Almost as quickly, he'd unzipped his pants so that it became obvious what he wanted her to do.

But she had no intention of playing his game and simply turned her back on him lying on her side.

He'd stood up. Was he going to leave? Instead, she heard one shoe, then the other drop on the floor. And then he was in bed beside her, holding her from behind, one hand on her breast.

Slowly she felt his hips working against her bottom. She tried to remain rigid, but as her fingers stroked her nipple, she felt her own hips responding.

"I guess it's all right if you come in my sheets."

"Wouldn't it be easier if I just came in your mouth."

"Noble!" She turned quickly in his arms, sat up, and shook her finger at him. "Behave."

He responded by taking her right nipple in his mouth and sucking long and hard upon it.

She shut her eyes. His hand went between her legs and she let him put it there, writhing as his fingers probed inside and rubbed against her clitoris.

Abruptly, he stopped. She wanted more and reached for his hand. Instead, he put her hand on his penis and at the same time, pushed down on her shoulders so that all she could see was his broad chest and then his jutting black cock.

"Put your mouth in front of it. I'll squirt inside; there won't be a mess or anything."

"Noble." How thoughtful you are, she thought and how selfish. Perhaps I wanted it between my legs, too. But she did not say what she was thinking, did not grab his fingers and place them back inside her.

Instead as his penis dark and throbbing advanced toward her waiting mouth, she closed her lips and held his prick at bay an inch or two away from her face. Wrong, she thought, wrong. He lost control at her touch and his newly released cum splashed across her mouth and chin, her mouth opening only to accept the last of it.

He used the sheet to guide the facial into her mouth, the edge of his palm scooping up the portion that had fallen across her breasts. "It'll make them even more beautiful," he said, echoing what her husband had once said to her years before on her honeymoon.

And then he was gone, off to school, while she lay back on the pillows and wondered how long it would be before she guided him inside her.

The Next Day

The next morning, again she woke unexpectedly, thinking, no, I locked the door, I'm sure I locked the door.

But Noble was inside her bedroom, laying his schoolbooks down on the floor. Again, he came toward her, deliberately undoing his fly.

"I told you no," she said, "We're not going to do this any more." And when he continued to walk toward her side of the bed, she deliberately turned away and stared steadfastly at the opposite wall.

Pictures of her daughter were hung there; one was an oil painting, but most were photographs: Megan at soccer practice, Megan running along a track, Megan in a school play.

Noble's weight settled heavily on the bed behind her. His arm wrapped around her body and he took her breast in his hand, his fingers toying lightly with her nipple. "No," she thought, "No." But she said nothing. She knew nothing she said would persuade him to move away. "You have to go to school," she whispered as she felt his clothed body cupping hers, his jeans rough against her skin.

She heard his zipper open further, could feel his penis hard against her buttocks. He slid down the bed and she could feel it between her legs, its tip only inches from her opening. He began to move against her; at the same time, his hand, which had already slid down from her breast, had reached the upper lip of her vagina where he rested one finger, its tip barely grazing the tip of her clitoris.

She gave a shudder, moaned happily, and adjusted her own position, so that his penis though still outside her body would rub against her. The finger was now inside her vagina; it made tiny circles enlarging the opening. "Please," she said, not sure at all what she meant.

He was nuzzling her shoulder with his lips. His long member traveling the width of her thigh with each thrust. She tried to turn toward him, but he had already come and her thighs, the sheets, her buttocks were covered with his fluid and her own. She turned then, held his head to her breasts, embraced him, and held him tightly with arms and thighs willing him not to go.

But far too soon he stood up, and wiped his now flaccid member on his embroidered pillowcase. Then with his fingers, he wiped some of his cum from her thighs and held it to her lips. She sucked on his fingers greedily, hoping against hope that he would stay with her.

But he had picked up his book bag, opened the sliding glass doors, and was gone.

Velma

While Marge quite often gave high teas at which everyone dressed up, mornings she would usually spend in the company of her cousin Millie or her friend Velma. The two seldom came together. Jo could guess why:

Marge's cousin and Velma were from two different worlds. One could see Millie doing church work, singing in the choir, or helping pass the collection plate. Velma belonged in a strip show.

And it didn't take much to get Velma to strip, or at least to take off her blouse and exhibit those store-bought breasts of hers.

"Size isn't all that matters," Marge said to Velma one morning after she had done just that. "Jo has extremely beautiful breasts and they're quite small."

Jo blushed. She was flattered but she hoped Millie would let the whole subject drop.

"She has, do she? Let's see them then."

"We're not all exhibitionists."

"Maybe her titties are false, too."

They definitely are not, Jo wanted to scream, but held her tongue. Surely, the three of them could find something else to talk about.

"My son Nobel has lots of pictures of Jo on his wall. I don't see any there of you."

Grateful for Marge's support, Jo still hoped they would let the whole subject drop and above all that they wouldn't go into

Nobel's room to look at the pictures. She was sure he had taken home one of her brassieres the day before. Hopefully, he would not have left it out where the others could see it. She would have to get it back from him. Maybe she'd have a chance later that morning.

She started to get up, but Marge held her back. Velma was talking once more, though braying would be a better description. "If he likes hers," she said, "It's 'cause he ain't had a chance to be wit a big woman's."

Amazingly, for it was not like Marge at all, Marge had begun to unbutton her own blouse. In a moment, both her blouse and her brassiere were on the carpet. "I show you big," she said.

Marge's breasts weren't merely big, Jo thought, they were astronomical, double D's with huge dark aureoles and enormous brown nipples. If she were to ever have sex with a woman, Marge would be the one.

"What about her," Velma asked, "Miss Fancy Pants. Is she going to keep her clothes on or is she go' in' to show us these wonderful titties you been raving about."

"She can keep her clothes on if she wants," Marge said loyally, but it was too late. Jo had known a girl just like Velma in the eighth grade. The other girl had made fun of Jo; Jo had unbuttoned her blouse; the other girl had not. She and two other girls then sat on the little bitch, pulling up her sweater, revealing the four pairs of socks that lay beneath.

"They something all right." Velma said once Jo's bra and blouse lay on the carpet next to Marge's. She came and stood next to Jo. Don't you touch me, Jo thought, don't you dare. But Velma had already taken Jo's hand and led her to stand in front of the now sitting Marge. "Which pair you want to suck," she said to Marge, and stuck out her chest placing her body side by side with Jo's. Too easy, Jo thought, your nipples are a good six inches closer to Marge's mouth than mine.

But Marge had reached out both her large brown hands, and had taken a breast from each of them. This is crazy, Jo thought, as an electric thrill went through her. Marge released Jo's breast barely brushing the nipple as she did so; then she took Jo's hand and placed it on her own large bosom.

Bent over awkwardly above where Marge sat on the couch, Jo had no choice but to kneel in front of her. Marge grasped Jo's breast a second time, her other hand on Jo's neck guiding her forward.

In a moment, Marge's large brown nipple was in Jo's mouth and she was sucking for all she was worth. At the same time, Velma's arms snaked around her body,

Velma's hands caressed her breasts. Velma's stiff nipples pressed against her back.

While Marge's right hand held Jo's head firmly against her breast, her other had snaked between Jo's legs, pulled aside her panties and begun to stroke within.

Jo heard a buzz, and then experienced a throbbing vibration in her anus, as Velma thrust the vibrator inside her. She struggled but was unable to move, her mouth filled with Marge's nipple and breast, Marge's fingers moving gently inside her. Jo came once, twice trying but unable to free herself from the vibrator.

The next moment, both women were nursing at her bosoms and she had yet another orgasm.

Afterward, she ate Marge's pussy while Velma ate hers. And then, without being asked, she made love to Velma starting with her firm hard breasts, trailing a string of kisses down Velma's belly, ending with her tongue in Velma's crotch, her ass cheeks up in the air while Marge gently probed her with the vibrator.

Late Night Telephone Call

That afternoon and the next, Jo might have wished for Noble's appearance at her door for a return to normalcy. What she had done the day before, what had been done to her should surely not be counted as normal no matter how much she may have enjoyed it.

But Noble did not come. She had glimpsed him once the previous day in the late afternoon, dragging an athletic bag along with his schoolbooks, but he had not come to her house but had gone straight home. Nor had he come over after supper. Not that she would have let him in the door.

That afternoon, while she was showing a client a relatively new listing, she had seen him walking along in the company of an over-endowed schoolgirl almost his own age. The two were holding hands. This should not have bothered her, but it did.

She wanted him to find someone his own age, of course, but she had supposed it would be someone more like her. Noble was always going about how beautiful her small breasts are, caressing them, and then his hand between her legs bringing her to orgasm, while her own hand held his swelling cock.

She was lying in her bed that night, thinking about this once again, fantasizing herself as that young girl she'd imagined, almost but not quite asleep when the phone rang. "Who is it?" she asked dreamily, when the caller did not speak up immediately.

"It's Noble."

"How are you?" she said, knowing at once that this was a stupid thing for her to say.

"I'm fine. Did you miss me?"

Not, "I missed you," but "Did you miss me?"

"I suppose. How have you been?" Her words were polite but distant, just as she had planned to be when and if he called.

"They give us lots of homework," he said, "and coach makes us practice longer. I gots no time. Did your titties miss me?"

They missed you very much, she thought, but she was not about to tell him that.

"Maybe you could coach me?" he continued

Coach him? At what? At tittie sucking he was a master. Unconsciously, her hand had gone down to her breast and begun to play with and knead the flesh.

"You know, history, math. I needs a B-average or I can't play."

"That girl you were with today; maybe she could help you." An instant vision of the big-bosomed slut he'd been walking hand-in-hand with that afternoon came to her.

"Katisha? She just a fren."

This was not what Jo had asked though it was what she had wanted to know.

"You want me to come over, suck your titties?"

Yes, no. Of course, she had to tell him no.

"No, it's much too late." She hadn't meant to say that. What she ought to have said was, no, we're not going to do that any more.

"Mom says you need to have your titties sucked regularly."

"Your mother told you that!" Jo was horrified.

"No, I hear her talking to Aunt Millie."

That was better then, or was it. Jo didn't like the fact that Marge had been talking about her at all. Not after what they had done together.

"I gonna do something else for you. Something women like, something Katisha told me to do."

"What?" She shouldn't have asked that. She should have hung up. But her hand had gone creeping down to her groin and she had begun to rub herself letting the sound of Noble's voice carry her away.

"I gonna eat your pussy."

"Oh, my God." She'd said it aloud into the telephone. Her hips were starting to move now, responding to the movements of her fingers.

"You like my taste."

"What?"

"The taste of my sperm. You like it?"

Why were they talking on the phone? Why didn't he come over? "It's O.K." she said weakly.

"Say you like the taste of my sperm. Say you want my big black cock."

"I ... like ... your ... big ... black ... cock." And then she was having a long sustained orgasm. From the sounds on the telephone, he was having one too. But he did not come over. Eighteen-year-old boys who live with their parents are not always free to do what they would like.

An Instructional Film

When the phone range at ten that morning and Marge White invited her over, Jo knew she would go next door no matter what she had promised herself.

"Just a little hen party."

After what had happened two days before, when she had lost all control of her body had done unthinkable things, had done them, not with a man, but with a woman, with two women, she had resolved to stay clear of the Whites. If Marge needed a favor, all right. She would loan her a cup of sugar or accept packages when Marge was not home. But she could never, never let herself do what she had done. But she'd loved what they made her do while they were doing it, had hated it only afterward.

When Noble came by on his way to school that morning, Jo was already up and dressed. When he slipped inside the house, through the locked rear door that he was somehow always able to open, she stepped out through the front and began to water the lawn. Ten minutes, fifteen passed and then he had no choice but to leave and go to school if he was not to be late.

She noticed that he chose to slip back out the back way, the way he had come, and realized that he, too, was afraid his mother might see him.

"Just a little hen party." Marge had said.

Jo dressed carefully, rejecting the first clothes she had chosen as inappropriate. She could not afford to dress in any manner that might suggest that she would want a repetition of what had taken place the day before. And yet that was precisely what she had done, her unconscious directing her hand first toward a white lace bra and a slit skirt. Carefully, methodically, glad that Noble was not there to watch her dress and undress, she'd taken them off and put the bra back in the drawer and the skirt in the closet.

Then, she dressed as she always did on workdays in basic realtor—a conservative dress with straight skirt and modest neckline, and a pushup support bra.

Whatever her body might desire would not show outwardly.

Marge was not alone, nor had she said she would be. Millie and a second older friend were with her, and not, Jo was gratified to see, the dreadful Velma. Her anus tingled at the very thought that Velma might still come.

"We're going to see a movie," Marge announced to her surprise and they all trekked into the family room where the big-screen TV was located.

A coffee-pot and cake were already on the table and Marge made sure they all had a cup and plate in front of them before she turned on the TV with her remote.

"It's instructional." Marge said.

But these were not quite the instructions Jo had expected. Instead, the apparent documentary began to provide step-by-step instructions on sucking a man's cock illustrated by a black woman sucking on a white man's penis and a white woman obliging a male Negro.

The film was frightening, disturbing, and fascinating at one and the same time. Jo was unwilling neither to take her eyes from the screen nor to make face-to-face contact with the other women.

She learned the corn cob—an action whereby the black woman moved her jaw slowly along the white man's penis nibbling at the sides as if his penis held a row of kernels, and the ice cream cone—which Jo had never seen before, the white woman licking the head and side of the black man's enormous penis as if it were a huge chocolate ice cream cone.

Her eyes left the screen only once as she brushed an invisible crumb from her lap, checking as unobtrusively as she could at the same time to be sure that the liquid from her now sopping pussy had not stained her realtor's dress.

The images on the screen halted abruptly as Marge hit the remote control. "The next part is the best," Marge said, "circular breathing."

"You've got to use circular breathing," the older woman counseled, "Otherwise, it's just not possible." She smiled indulgently at Jo who, embarrassed, quickly looked down again at her lap.

"Circular breathing," the motherly looking woman on the screen explained was simply a technique by which the woman could suck and swallow continually without overflow. Strangely, a white man sucking on a black man's cock illustrated this part of the film, which Jo thought was disgusting.

The film ended and surprisingly Marge and her older friend both briefly applauded.

"Lordy, it's been a long time," the older woman said. "You?" She turned to Jo.

"She's a widow," Marge interjected, "but I'm sure she's got great memories. 'Bout time you dated though, Girl Friend."

Jo tried to look properly horrified. "I'd have to know someone really well first."

"But you're not against it." The older woman said. Without waiting for an answer, she added, "I heard white women were too prissy about that sort of thing. That's why white men are always looking for black pussy."

Jo looked and was shocked. But she wasn't sure what she could say in her defense. You're wrong; I sucked my husband's cock a hundred times and my high school sweetheart's, too.

"Ever suck a black man's?"

Jo's face turned bright red.

"Jo, you're blushing."

"Black man's tastes as good as a white's."

"Maybe more to swallow though."

"Depends on the man's," Marge said loyally.

"What you think, girl?" said the older women, "Jo-Jo, that your name."

"Alma, you are embarrassing her."

"No, I've never," Jo said, then added, afraid the woman might think she was prejudiced, "not that I would object, I mean if the right man...the right black man"

Mildred laughed, a rich full laugh that filled the room. "I dunno, small mouth like yours, you might never get it all in."

"Mildred." The two black women began to argue, but Jo was not listening. She could think only of the many times she had wanted to take Noble's cock in her mouth, had stopped only because stimulated by her hand he had already come. He was just too young. She had to get a boy friend, start dating as Marge suggested, find someone quickly before she went all the way with an eighteen-year old boy.

At Home with the Whites

A fly on the wall would have enjoyed the conversation at the Whites the next morning.

Husband and wife were having an argument at the breakfast table, though it was a friendly argument. "Has he fucked her yet?" Mr. White wanted to know.

"Puleese."

"The boy tells me she hasn't even given him a proper blow job. Now, if we'd done things my way."

"We are not going to do things your way. That was the agreement. If we hadn't done things your way before, Roland would not be in the Marines now, would be home safe where I would not have to worry about him."

"What does one thing have to do with another?" Disgusted, Mr. White tried to take a gulp of coffee, lest he say the wrong thing, only to discover his cup was empty. "More coffee, woman."

Marge White pointed silently to the electric percolator. Mr. White tromped heavily across the floor as he walked toward it. He was as big in his way as Marge White was in hers—a torn knee cartilage was all that had kept him from a pro football career, and his anger was apparent in each step. Marge White proceeded to make her point.

"Noble is my son. Roland was your son. You messed up with Roland, now we're going to do things right."

∙∙∙

Mr. White's method of sex education had been far more direct than his wife's.

Having noticed as his wife had, that his older son was particularly attracted to what then had been their next-door neighbor, he'd made a quick study of their neighbor's habits, then struck one day with the lightning efficiency that characterized each of his business deals.

As with Jo, he'd only a nodding acquaintance with the neighbor, would have a hard time remembering her name today, even though for a period of time, she'd become an integral part of his family's life.

Susan had not been a particularly attractive woman, not that Mr. White found white women particularly attractive. She was dowdy, soft, with breasts that innumerable departing children had presumably sucked, and a peculiar walk that suggested too much time in chairs, too little in beds or on the golf course.

Her clothes shouldn't have tempted anyone—old ragged sweaters, long gray skirts, sweatshirts with causes emblazoned on them, and pants she should never have worn. He suspected that the attraction she held for Roland, then only 18 and as shy as his younger brother would later prove to be, was that she was there, she had breasts, and she wasn't his mother. "And she's got a vagina," Mr. White had thought, "That's all she needs to get the boy started."

Susan, her name went with her gray skirts, liked to take walks. A wooded area lay at the end of their street still waiting for the developers and she could be expected to take a walk there at least once a week through the meadow and on to the next housing tract.

One afternoon, five years before, when she set out across the fields, Mr. White and Roland were right behind her. She smiled at them—Mr. White carried a picnic basket and with Roland by his side, certainly looked harmless—and waited for them to catch up. "I'm your neighbor," she began, as if Mr. White did not know that already.

Roland had skipped ahead, annoyed that his solitary walk with his father should be interrupted by another adult.

Which gave Roland's father the opportunity he'd been waiting for. "Take off your bra," he whispered in Susan's ear. Coming as the whisper did from a full head above where Susan's ear was from a man solid and broad across the shoulders as any two men, his command was very effective. Indeed, along with the knife he showed her lying across the top of the picnic basket it yielded an immediate response.

She'd quickly slipped the brassiere out from beneath her sweater, a cup at a time, and handed it to him. In an instant, it had disappeared inside the basket. "What else do you want me to do?" she'd asked. It was clear he had gotten her full attention.

"I want you to breast feed my son.

Roland, come back here. This is our next-door neighbor; I want you to take her hand, walk with her. I'm going to walk by myself over here out of the way." He looked at Susan and the look said what he'd no need to say aloud, "If you run away, I'll catch you and cut off your nipples."

The two had walked away hand in hand, Mr. White following off to the side and slightly behind so they would not need to see or even think about him. At least, Roland would not.

The woman from next door looked back over her shoulder once and only once. Then Roland's hands had gone beneath her sweater, had undone the buttons. They had seated themselves on the ground—Mr. White was behind a tree now, so that he could see but not be seen. Roland was attacking one of the woman's breasts. Susan spoke to the boy, though her words could not be made out over the distance, and he grew calmer though no less passionate. Roland soon pushed her to the ground, let his mouth be guided to the woman's other breast. "She's goin' t'have one sore titty," Mr. White thought. Then Roland's hand was underneath the woman's skirt, had forced his way between her legs. She began to move uncontrollably, to make little cries. Roland's hips thrust in and out as well, though as Mr. White noted, "the damn fool still has his pants buttoned."

Then both figures lay quietly on the grass and to Mr. White's surprise, Susan took Roland's head in her hands and kissed him.

Time for lunch, he thought, and walked toward the couple. "Lunch," he said when he was close to them. To his amazement, Roland bounded up and interposed himself between his father and the still prone women. He helped her to her feet, and then glared at his father.

Whatever. Mr. White led them farther on to a grassy area that lay below a hillside of piled rocks. Here, he removed a table cloth from the basket, spread it open, placed two wrapped sandwiches and two cokes on it, and then, because his son clearly thought him an intruder, removed a final sandwich and beverage and carried them with him up the hillside to the shelter of the rocks.

Looking down, he could see that Roland had removed his jacket and spread it for the woman to sit upon. "All that fuss," he thought, " and she the only one to get her pleasure."

When finished his own sandwich, he'd strolled down to where the couple were deep in conversation. "Excuse me son," he'd said, and then bent down to whisper in the Susan's ear again. "You had your pleasure. Now, I expect you to take his weapon out and give Roland his. Unless, you want to see mine." He gestured toward the picnic basket, then smiling at Roland, he bent down over Susan a second time, "Unzip him, now."

She did as she was told, Roland neither helping nor hindering. When she held Roland's penis in her hand, Mr. White said, "Press her head down, son, she needs direction." Roland did as he was told, cupping the woman's breast in the same motion. Mr. White happily strolled back up the hill.

Afterward, he led them out toward the second housing tract where he'd parked the touring car earlier that day. He opened the rear door and motioned them both inside. "I be back," he said and motioned them within.

There was a property on this street that he'd had his eye on for some time, and Mr. White was not one to forgo business for pleasure. Still he was pleased as he returned to the car to find the woman's head again buried in his son's lap and Roland with a by-now-familiar look of ecstasy on his face.

Mr. White had strolled back up the street a dozen steps or so—it wouldn't take long for them to finish, he knew, then returned and stepped into the car, deliberately not looking into the rear seat.

On their return, he stopped the car for a moment in front of the woman's driveway. She got out and when Roland made a move to close the door behind her, Mr. White stopped him. "No. You walk her to her door, see that she's safe inside."

Roland had not returned home that evening, though Mrs. Rensk had called to say she was fixing dinner for him. He did not return home that night either and from then on, until he left home entirely at age 18, he had continued to enjoy the woman's favors.

She had been pregnant with Roland's child when she had gone ahead to the town where Roland was to have gone to college, gone ahead to set up a house for the two of them.

Mrs. White had not been happy with the extended relationship, and was extremely unhappy when Roland crossed both her and Mrs. Rensk up and joined the Marines.

Things were going to be done her way with Jo and Nobel. Slow and sure. And her husband knew he was not to interfere.

Dessert.

The very next evening after Marge had shown Jo the film, Marge called to invite her to supper.

"I've already eaten."

"Then come for dessert. About seven."

Seven o'clock came and she'd walked over to the White's dressed in a proper blouse, a hard bra beneath—there was to be no fooling around, and jeans that would defy all attempts to slip a hand inside them.

The White's kitchen was filled with a delicious aroma. The dessert was to be homemade pie then.

The kitchen was also replete with teenage angst. "I don't want to go." she heard Nobel say.

"That's not an option young man." was his mother's reply.

Hands on her ample hips, Marge turned to Jo. "Just what am I going to do with him."

"I'm sure Nobel wants to be helpful." Jo smiled. Noble looked pleased, discomfited, and angry all at the same time. A teenager.

"She wants me to go to the store."

"To get ice cream."

"Don't you want ice-cream?" Again, Jo smiled, then again wished she hadn't. She was flirting and she wanted to be stern to let Noble know that they were going to remain at a distance from now on.

"Will you go with me?" His face was that of an abandoned cocker spaniel. Of course she would go with him. "Of course, I will."

Their walk started out with him several steps ahead of her. Gradually, he dropped back until, when they were a block or two from his house, he was walking next to her, his thigh brushing against hers with each step.

Just as well I wore the jeans, she thought.

At the drug store, they bought a brick of vanilla, though at first, Nobel had picked up chocolate.

"Not with pie," she'd said.

Over her objections, he bought himself a chocolate cone. He offered her one, but she turned it down. "Later with the pie." But a half block later, when he offered her a lick, she accepted.

They were walking like that, taking turns with the cone, when she realized they'd left the pavement and had headed into the woods that lay between the strip mall and her house.

"Where are we going?" she asked.

"Short cut." A short cut, huh. Well, he'd find the clothes she was wearing a barrier to any mischief he had planned. But Nobel had planned something different altogether.

"You like chocolate," he asked.

"Yes," she answered and started to babble again about the pie when she looked down to where he was pointing.

His black penis protruded a good six inches from his pants front.

"Nobel, we're out in public."

"Nobody here but the birds and they's don't care."

Nobody was there under the trees but the birds, no one to see her lick the cone. She needed to walk away, but he held her by the shoulders.

"Please."

She really shouldn't, but she had already knelt, gathering the leaves beneath her knees for comfort, and begun to lick. Her mouth traveled up and down and around the head of his penis. At first, she could visualize the woman in the movie, and then she was that woman, and then his hand was behind her head supporting her as he came convulsively. She swallowed as much as she could without gagging, took a breath, and then swallowed some more, licking the last few drops from the tip.

The woman in the film had said it would take several attempts to master circular breathing.

Jo stood up, forgetting to brush the pine needles from her knees, and tried to kiss him. He turned his mouth away. "You kiss me," she insisted. And he did.

A quick glance at Jo's clothes when the pair returned and then again at the clock, convinced Marge that everything was going according to plan. Her husband's way had only acquired a woman for their oldest son; her way would ultimately yield a sex slave for the entire family.

Marge's Brother

One member of Marge's family, Jo hadn't met was Marge's brother.

He'd been described variously by Marge's friends as "dreamy," "super handsome," or "you've simply got to meet him." Jo wasn't quite sure how she would react if she did meet him. To be brutally honest, Marge was her first and only African-American friend. She'd never dated a black man and Jo wasn't quite sure she would want to.

She was sure Marge sensed her hesitation as unlike Marge's friends, Marge didn't go gushing on about her brother, though she seemed to enjoy matchmaking when the two were out together, suggesting half-jokingly that perhaps some young waiter or a bewildered looking male who'd wandered by chance into a section of a department store set aside for woman's clothing would make an ideal mate for her.

"I'm happy being alone," Jo would say, but, of course, Jo wasn't and Marge knew it.

The night Jo met Marge's brother, Marge's house was filled with company. There'd been a barbecue on the back lawn; Jo hadn't had much more than salad, though the rest of the guests ate heartily, and Jo was always being offered meat, usually by a married man whose wife would be quick to follow and pull him away.

Noble lurked in the background, looking forlorn, and staring at Jo whenever he felt she wasn't looking back at him. Jo knew this because Velma, Marge's truly annoying single friends, was quick to point it out. "Another year older," Velma said to her, "And maybe Jo better take care of his needs 'fore someone else does. You best hurry." A statement no more outrageous than the ones Velma usually made.

When Jo asked why Velma bothered to hang around, for as far as Jo could see Noble was the only single man at Marge's party, she said, "I's waiting for Reggie. He s'posed to be coming. He is so handsome. I could just eat him up."

"You already tried that," Marge interjected sneaking up on them, for as a good hostess she seemed to be everywhere at once. "He was just too much for you to swallow."

"Ain't that the truth."

Jo was the only one of the three of them to blush though she'd yet to meet the brother.

After everyone had eaten, the crowd on the lawn gradually melted away. Most of the couples excusing themselves to go home or to a movie or to wherever they planned to spend the rest of the evening, while Mr. White and his cronies disappeared into the basement to watch a taped game on the TV.

This left Velma and Marge and Jo alone on the lawn, along with Noble who was swinging on the door to the house until he was instructed by his mother to go finish his homework.

They heard him holler "Uncle Reggie," as he turned to step inside the house and then Marge's brother put in his appearance on the lawn.

He was exceptionally attractive, tall, handsome, and broad shouldered, though not overly muscular as Mr. White was and as his son was gradually becoming, more like a tennis pro than a football player.

In fact, he had been playing tennis. This was what had kept him. That and a long shower afterward. "I'd like to have seen that," said Velma, but he didn't rise to the bait.

Velma and Marge scurried to fix him a plate of food from the leavings of the barbecue, but it seemed he had eyes only for Jo.

He talked almost exclusively with her while he ate, small talk, the casual conversation any couple are liable to have on a first date.

Jo amused herself by wondering if he would try to kiss her sometime that evening and thought yes, Jo will kiss him back. They were in Mr. White's study a half hour or so later when he did try. They kissed and then his hand reached up and pulled her blouse out of his skirt. Jo said, "Aren't we going just a little bit fast."

He did not reply, but instead sat down behind the desk in Mr. White's big chair where he sat for a few moments, studying her, his eyes roaming over every part of her body. "Come here," he said finally.

She inched closer and then, abruptly, he reached out and pulled her into his lap. She tried to get up, but the position was awkward and he was very strong. Besides, when he kissed her again, she kissed him back.

Only when he began to unbutton her blouse, did she start to struggle and then, with both her hands clasped behind her back in one of his, there was not much she could do. Jo looked all around for help and saw that the door to the study was open.

Well, he's not going to rape me, she thought. "If you don't stop, I'll scream," she said.

"You ever kiss a black man before? No, you don't mind the kissing." He kissed her again, releasing her hands. Automatically, these had risen to embrace his head. She loved the feel of his curly black hair.

The kissing went on for some time, his hands sliding up under her blouse again and pushing away her bra. She said, "No," but he had her nipple in his mouth and then her entire breast.

His hand went between her legs but she pressed her thighs firmly together and he seemed content to leave it there, mere inches from the target.

Coming up for air, he said, "You have gorgeous breasts."

"They're small," Jo said.

"But they're perfect. And you've got those wonderful freckles." And he proceeded to kiss every one of those freckles and Jo was starting to think shouldn't we close the study door and then, shouldn't we stop, wait for a second date or a third.

"You ever make love to a black man? Suck his cock."

"I don't intend to make love to one now."

She couldn't believe what he'd said about his cock, about sucking it. She hadn't said "No" because he was black, but because they'd only just met and they'd already gone too far. Besides, he really wasn't black as Marge White and her husband were black, but was more of a cafe-au-lait color.

'You probably think all us black men carry straight razors." And the next moment Jo was looking at her reflection in the long sharp blade of the razor that he'd removed from his jacket pocket. He held the razor close to her jaw, then brought it along the curve of her neck, down, down until it nestled against the breast he'd nuzzled only a few moments before. Momentarily, she stopped breathing.

"Be terrible to cut this off," he said.

Jo looked all about her, saw the open doorway, and thought someone will come by; they'll see me; they'll stop him.

"You pretty much of a tease," he said.

She shook her head. "I didn't mean to be."

"Gets me all excited and then you jess want to walk away like that."

She shook her head again.

He pushed the chair back another foot from the desk. "Get down on your knees," he said, spreading his legs apart at the same instant so that Jo dropped to the ground. She tried to pull away but he'd grabbed her hair.

"Unzip me," he said, then added, "be careful." as his long bronze-black penis jumped into view.

This isn't happening, she thought.

He gestured with the knife. "You know what to do."

Jo put her lips down to the head of his penis thinking it will all be over soon.

"No!"

Jo jerked her head up. What was wrong?

"You gots to get to know Sam first. Take Sam in your hand."

His penis was long and heavy, thicker than her late husband's. She didn't know how she would ever get it all in her mouth. She began to stroke it slowly; maybe he would come before she had to suck on it.

"No! Rub it against your cheek, like it was a chile. Get to know it. She stroked her cheek with his penis, rubbed against it like a cat. Sam, the name he had given his penis, was soft, smooth.

"Now kiss it, up and down."

Jo brought her head inside his pants and kissed the shaft just above where it emerged from his body, raining down a series of little kisses along its length until she reached the head.

Then she did the same on the other side of the shaft, using her tongue now along with her lips.

She was no longer in control or thinking about escape or of how soon he would come but of how beautiful his penis was, how she would so much rather have it inside her vagina then in her mouth. Grabbing the shaft between her hands and opening her mouth as wide as possible, she tried to swallow as much of him as she could, stopping only when she was on the edge of choking.

"Slow."

But Jo didn't need to be told. Slowly, she brought Sam out of her throat and mouth until she was able to run her tongue over and along its head. As his cum came jetting out, she let it fill her throat, swallowing all she could. But still it came, pouring out of her mouth, dripping down on her blouse and cheeks, her freckled breasts.

Was he trying to get away? She would not let him. She slid her mouth down his shaft as far as she could, her hands on his testicles gripping him tightly.

"Gently, gently," Jo heard Reggie's deep voice from far away outside her. In the end, it was he who pulled her head away, face filled with pride. "You wonderful," he said. He buttoned his pants after which he pulled a handkerchief from his pocket and carefully wiped first her face and then her chest where the drops of his sperm still clung and brought it up to her lips to lick.

He stood up then and walked from the room.

Jo was sitting in the chair behind the desk where Reggie had sat a moment before when Marge and Velma walked into the room.

"He raped me," Jo said.

"Who did?" they asked together.

"Your brother. Marge's brother. He didn't rape me in the usual way. He forced me to go down on him."

"Forced you?"

"Yes. He had a knife. I mean a razor, a straight razor."

"Honey we didn't see no razor." Marge said.

"She think all niggers got a straight razor," said Velma.

"You saw?" Jo stammered.

"Course we saw," Velma said, "Door was wide open. You goin' to pleasure yourself, you should be more discreet. And we didn't see no woman being forced."

"What we saw," Marge said, "was a woman in love."

"What we saw," Velma added, "was a woman in love with a big black cock. Man, you cradled it like a baby, then you rained kisses all up and down it and when you gets to sucking on it finally, why you wouldn't let go."

Marge drew her to her feet. "Jo, you shouldn't be ashamed of being a woman or of making love to a black man."

"Reggie is one handsome dude."

They didn't believe her. How could this be possible? He'd raped her.

"Do you want to go home now or do you want to stay and watch T.V?"

"Go home," Jo said.

Marge walked her friend to the front door. "Do you want me to go home with you?"

Jo gestured toward her own house just the other side of the hedge separating the two properties. "I'll be O.K."

The door closed behind her. "Tomorrow," she'd said. Yes, tomorrow. Tonight, Jo would take a shower, throw her panties in the clothes hamper—they were soaked with her juices, along with her skirt, her blouse and what remained of her bra.

As Jo rounded the hedge, Marge's son Noble suddenly popped into view.

"Why'd you let him do that?" he said. "I love you and you won't even let me touch you. He don't love you."

"That's not true," Jo said. "You know, it's not."

"Kiss me," he ordered.

"I'm not sure that's such...."

"Kiss me." Jo let him kiss her, let him put his hands on her breasts and caress them, let him lead her to her own front door. Jo handed him her key. He opened the door and followed her in.

What happened next was predictable. First, he kissed her, then he sucked on her breasts, each of them in turn, uttering nonsense love words which she could not distinguish. Then she was kneeling in front of him taking his penis in her mouth. There was no opportunity for love making as there had been with Reggie though Jo felt she owed Noble as much or more than she'd given Marge's brother. He came quickly, his cum spurting everywhere as much on her rug and on her clothes as in her mouth. Then he had left the house and as Jo had planned she made her way slowly along the hall toward the promised shower.

Marge Reads Jo The Riot Act

When Marge invited her to come swimming at her home the next day, Jo reluctantly accepted.

Marge had not believed her. The night before, Jo had been raped, forced to suck a black man's cock. Never mind that he was Marge's brother; if Marge truly had been Jo's friend, she would have believed her and not him. Though, if it what Marge (and Velma, too) had said they'd seen the night before were true, then Jo couldn't blame them for thinking she'd made it all up.

Jo knew she'd lost control at some point that evening and had gone on to suck that big brown cock long after the straight razor had been taken away.

For the moment, she would assume this was what Marge and Velma had seen, that Marge had no choice but to believe her brother rather than her friend.

Still, she was not prepared for Marge to read her the riot act that morning, to welcome her to her home with abuse rather than friendship.

Jo had crossed the lawns between their two houses wearing only a skimpy bikini, a suit she would never wear in public, only in the privacy of her own pool or, as the case that morning, with a close friend.

With only the bikini and a towel flung over her bare shoulder, she felt vulnerable and naked in the face of Marge's accusations.

"You had sex with my son. He's just sixteen.

I could go to the police, have you arrested."

Jo was taken aback, frightened at the mention of police. What was Marge referring to? The walk in the woods Jo had taken with Noble to get ice cream two nights ago? The many afternoons she had spent with Noble on the couch after he got home? Had Marge listened in on their phone conversations? Or had she become aware only the night before when Noble had walked her home after the party?

"But you showed me the film. Please no, no police. I thought you knew."

"You thought I knew? What kind of a woman are you?" Marge's voice was filled with bitterness. But inside she was laughing at the frightened figure before her. On an impulse, she reached out and snapped off Jo's bikini top.

Jo recoiled, and then instinctively crossed her hands over her breasts.

"Millie was right," Marge said. "These needed attention. Every woman's does. I thought Noble would be good for you and you for him, but I never dreamed things would go this far."

Actually, Marge thought, I thought they'd have gone much further by this time, that boy of mine is so slow.

"Did he please you?"

Jo's mouth opened, but no words came out. What did Marge mean?

"I enjoyed breast feeding my childrens so much. Did you?"

Jo nodded. That memory at least was a pleasant one.

"That Noble, he practically sucked my titties off. Bet he made you feel good."

Jo smiled, and then realize this was the last thing she should be doing.

"Come with me," Marge said and walked toward the next room, still carrying Jo's bikini top.

Jo followed sheepishly and the next moment found herself in Marge's bedroom, that is, in the room that housed the bed Marge and Mr. White shared.

"He don't always please me," Marge said, alluding to her absent husband. She removed her own halter-top revealing the two large bare breasts beneath.

"You come here child."

"Shouldn't we..." Jo began, uncertain of what she wanted to say.

"Shouldn't we be going to the police station? I suppose we should. But I miss those children so. I want you to please me, now. I want you to come here and suck my tittie."

Jo did as she was told, practically smothering as Marge proceeded to force more and more of her enormous breast into Jo's mouth. When she could breathe again, it was because Marge's mouth had moved down to Jo's nipples, while Marge's fingers had reached beneath Jo's bikini bottoms and begun to stroke her clitoris.

It took only a few moments and Jo had her first orgasm. Then the bikini bottoms were removed, Marge's tongue replaced her fingers and Jo had her second.

"Now, it's your turn to please me." Marge said.

Marge really hadn't explained this part of her plan to her husband but then he didn't need to know everything. Besides, as Jo came to accept Marge as her lover she would be even more willing to welcome Noble.

The immensity of Marge's vagina was disconcerting, its taste even more so. Jo wondered if Marge had bothered to rinse after her husband came inside her that morning. Or did all black women taste this way?

They were in the pool, Marge in her bathing suit, Jo still without hers when Noble returned from lunch.

The subject of Jo and Noble together had been brought up only one more time. "You will not get pregnant," Marge had insisted. "You feel you need to pleasure yourself, you come see me."

Noble had no sooner stepped out on the patio, when his mother screamed at him. "Don't you know enough to knock? We're private out here. Go to your room and I'll tell you when lunch is ready."

When he'd left, clearly afraid of what his mother might do, she turned to Jo. "And now Missy, we'd best get you some clothes on. I fear that boy may have seen far too much of you."

After taking a quick shower off the master bedroom, Jo discovered that the bathing suit she'd walked over with had been replaced by the sweater she'd worn on her original date with Nobel and a very tight skirt. The skirt was a long one, which was just as well as neither brassier or panties were at hand.

After dressing, she found Nobel and his mother together in the kitchen. All the fixings for lunch were present but no lunch had actually been made. Apparently, Noble's mother had found a renewed scolding necessary.

"Darling," she said to Jo, "I've a hair appointment I forgot all about. Could you fix Noble his lunch?"

Jo couldn't really say no, though she wanted to. As expected, the minute the front door had closed on his mother, Nobel had her breasts in his hands. Never mind that she had a bread knife in hers.

"Don't you need to get back to school? " she whispered. Noble only followed through on his original attack, pulling her down to sit astride him at the kitchen table. In an instant, her nipple was in his mouth and his hand was busy beneath her skirt.

He removed the hand only to pull down on his zipper and that was when she acted, grabbing his hands in hers, pushing him back and kissing him full on the lips. They were locked in that same embrace when he came against her naked vulva, a full upward thrust that, thankfully, led to his load spilling inside his pants well away from the danger area.

"I can't get pregnant," she thought, repeating what Marge had insisted on earlier that day. Breasts, yes. Oral sex, yes. Anything further and something would have to be done. Mr. White would insist on it.

When Noble returned to the kitchen after changing his pants, his sandwich was made and on the table. Surprisingly, he sat down immediately and ate it, avoiding her, and drank a full glass of milk as well. He asked her for a second glass and she was on her way to get it, when he said, "I's going to drink this one off your titties."

She ignored his crudity. Though she spent a moment then and later thinking about what it would be like to have him lick and suck her milk-covered nipples. But they had no time for that. "We've got to go," what she said. "You'll be late for class otherwise."

"Can you drive me?"

"All right, but no funny business."

A minimum of funny business occurred on the trip to school, perhaps only because he could not afford to be late. Her mistake lay in agreeing to pick him up afterward.

He was not alone. Two other colored boys were with him. "They lives in the neighborhood," he said, "Can you gives them a lift, too?"

Her second mistake lay in agreeing to take the shortcut home he suggested. Surely with two other boys in the car, he wouldn't have anything else in mind. But the "shortcut" led to a secluded parking area with a view of the valley below. Not that she saw much of it.

His first demand was that she show the other boys her breasts. He'd promised them, he told her, that he'd show them what white girl looked like.

"I won't do that," she began, not liking where his request was leading.

"You making me look bad in front of my home boys," he hummed into her ear at the same time he fumbled with the buttons on her blouse.

"You'll rip it!" she protested trying to pull away.

"Just show them!"

Reluctantly, she unbuttoned her blouse; she'd paid too much for it at Nordstrom to allow it to be ripped.

"Show them."

She turned in her seat. Let them make what they wanted of her white lace bra and the hint of pink breasts above the lace.

"They's small," one of the boys said.

"They's not," Noble insisted and in an instant, he'd unsnapped her bra and lifted her bodily above the top of the seat so the boys could get a full view of her small bosoms.

She squirmed and tried to get away, but Noble was too strong.

One of the boys reached out a hand and cupped a breast. "They fine," he said. The other went directly to the source, fitting his mouth over the nipple of the remaining breast and began to suck.

She gave an inadvertent moan. Before she could protest, the first boy had begun to suck on the remaining nipple. He was far from gentle. "You're hurting."

"You're hurting her man, ease up."

The pain ceased. The sucking continued for several months with Jo leaning farther and farther over the back of the seat until, finally, the two boys had enough and released her.

Noble opened the door of the car. "You come now," he said to her. She followed, uncertain where she was going or what they were going to do.

Hollering over his shoulder to the two boys to "waits in the car, like I said," he proceeded after a few strides to disappear into the bushes. Unthinkingly, she followed.

"None of their business, what we're going to do next;" he said to her, "suck your titties is the best they goin' to do."

She knelt then before him, knowing what he wanted, her small breasts still bobbing free of all confinement. It took only a minute or two to bring him to a climax, the chief problems being to avoid choking when he came and to be sure that she hadn't spilled any on her clothes.

He took his handkerchief then and carefully wiped around her chin. She was grateful for his attentions, unaware that he'd deliberately left a few drops of sperm loose on her breasts so his friends would know what they had done.

"I need a drink of water," she said.

"We go home now," was his only answer as they walked back to the car.

Morning, Noon, and Night

In the days that followed Jo could expect to wake each morning, give Noble her breasts so that he might suck them at his leisure or came against her thighs or her belly after which he went off to school.

An hour or so later, Mr. White's car would leave the garage, and the call would come from Marge. Jo would be obliged to spend her morning going down on the older woman, and only occasionally (not nearly as often as she would have liked) to have Marge go down on her.

At night when Nobel returned from school, he would stop by, fill her mouth with sperm and be off again. Once when he was late because he had sports, he called from school and asked her to pick him up. Of course, they took a shortcut and repeated everything they had done before. Though this time, he kept working on her with his hand while he sucked, until she had no choice but to come exhausted against him.

Jo was getting more and more aroused. But she could not ignore Marge's warning, or the threat of arrest hanging over her. "I mustn't get pregnant," she kept repeating. In case this incantation failed, she resolved to make an appointment as soon as possible with her gynecologist to get the pill.

Meanwhile, Marge had thought up her own method of birth control, one that would begin when Jo least expected it.

Happy Horrigan

Happy Horrigan, the realtor, was glad to see Jo. She was a good producer and each of her frequent sales meant more money for him.

"I wondered how long it would be before you got back."

"I needed the activity," she said, not adding that she needed something to keep her mind off waiting and wondering whether a fifteen-year old boy would be coming to her house that day after school and what he would want her to do. Doing with her pretty much whatever he felt like, she realized, and felt a slow warmth grow inside her.

Mr. Horrigan was staring at her. She needed to concentrate.

"The bandwagon is Tuesday morning as always," he said, "But if you like, I could take you around now, show you some of the new stuff."

He continued to stare. What was the reason? Happy was married. Happily, she'd always thought, though she was aware that he appreciated her as a woman as well as an awfully good salesman. She wondered if there was anything amiss in the clothes she was wearing. But of course when she looked down at her blouse and then at her skirt, his eyes naturally followed hers.

I'm spooked, she thought. This man just wants to help me get back in the business. I'm the only one here with sex on her mind.

"If you don't mind," she said, "I would like to get go. The sooner, the better."

"Just a few calls, first." he motioned her into a chair. She picked up a magazine, then thought, I ought to be looking at the listings. But when she started to get up, he waved her back. "Only be a moment."

Was he looking at her legs? She thought back to the previous year when she'd been working for him regularly, her husband still alive. Everything had been perfectly proper. He was the boss and her mentor. She was the new salesman and then, had it been just August of last year, she was salesman of the month.

She smiled at the memory, found him smiling back at her.

He pulled her to her feet then, and led her down the hall and out the back door to his big Mercedes, a twin to her own.

Of course, at the Christmas party that year, both of them slightly drunk, his hand had slipped up inside her bra to cup her breast. "They are small and perfect," Happy had said and kissed her ear before releasing her.

"How's Mrs. Horrigan," she asked and realized she was asking because she hoped that Mrs. Horrigan was no more, that Happy would once again cup her small breast in his hand.

He looked over puzzled before putting his eyes back on the road. "All tied up with her social work. Just as well. With the kids gone off to college, she was pretty much at loose ends for a while. You know how it is."

While they drove, she talked about her departed husband, how she felt she might be ready now to start dating. Then, their discussion went back to business. She wasn't sure if she were relieved or disappointed.

"This is a new development I want you to see.

"Colored guy put it together, but the construction's pretty decent, just a few corners cut here and there. We've got an exclusive for the next few months. Had to give a little on the commission but I think we can make up for it in volume."

Ten minutes later, they pulled up in front of a model home. After helping her out of the car, he reached into a back pocket and extracted a large ring of keys. She noticed as he did so that he was doing his best to hide a rather obvious erection. He does like me, she thought as he unlocked the model's door.

In a slightly louder voice as if leading a tour, he took her through the downstairs rooms. The model had been furnished with just enough chairs and tables to look lived in while leaving the impression of lots of available space. Good sales technique, she thought, doubly pleased hat she was now thinking like a real estate agent again instead of a sex mad virgin.

Happy led her up to the second floor of the model home and they stepped into what was unmistakably a master bedroom. A large four-poster bed complete with canopy occupied its corner.

Peek inside," he said, and held the canopy open for her. A linen bedspread, pink silk sheets and embroidered pillowcases. A woman's dream. She turned to share the thought with him and her breast was against his arm, his still-evident erection against her thigh.

"Anyone home up there," boomed a deep bass voice from the floor below. "I see yo car Horrigan. Hope you decent. Not messing about on that four-poster of mine."

Horrigan stepped away from her quickly. Jo tried to do the same, caught her knees on the bed frame, and had no choice but to sit back on the mattress.

They could hear heavy footsteps coming up the staircase and then, to Jo's surprise, Mr. White, Marge's husband entered the room.

"Sorry about that. Didn't realize," White said.

"She's an employee," Horrigan said as if somehow that explained things.

"My apologies to you Ma'am," White said to Jo, "I was just joking a moment ago. Only woman I ever caught Happy in here with was his daughter. Least I think she was his daughter.

"Just joking again," he added when he saw the look of their faces. He laughed, a deep booming laugh. A pleasant almost infectious laugh, Jo thought, but Horrigan didn't look as if he were amused.

Before Happy could speak, White continued talking, this time looking closely at Jo. "Wait a minute. Ain't you my next-door neighbor? Yeah, you Marge's friend. You Marge's close friend." He no longer looked as if he were happy. Turning to Horrigan, he asked," You with her."

"She's my employee," Happy repeated, stiffly.

"Well then Hell, she's on the team." White grasped Jo's small hand in his big one and pulled her to her feet. "Let me give you the tour."

"Been there, done that." Happy said.

"If you need to go..." Jo began, meaning to add, "I could come back another time."

"Let him go, then." White said, "I can drive you home good as him and with less trouble doing it."

The two men stared at each other for a moment, like two lions vying for sole possession of a piece of meat.

Finally, Horrigan realized who the larger lion was or at least who was going to let him make up on volume what had been lost on the individual commissions. "Well, if he's your next door neighbor...."

"I'm parked at your office." Jo said. "Horrigan real estate," she added turning to White.

"Not a problem," White said. "Long as you pay for the gas."

They completed the tour. Ever so often, White looked at her and said, "Marge's friend." He did not look happy when he said it.

He knows, Jo thought. But what's he mad about? She makes me do what he won't do for her.

Car Ride

They took off quickly in Mr. White's Cadillac, an older model
equipped with bench seats. She sat as far away from him on
the front seat as she possibly could. They did not head in the
direction of the real estate office.

"Got's to pick up the men first," White said, once again
deliberately slurring the words, playing at being colored.

The "men" were three burly, somewhat smelly workers, who'd
been working in a house on the far edge of the development.
"Their job is to clean up the rough edges, leave it spanking."
The sweat on the men's faces and their powerful aroma said
they'd been doing more than just polishing.

They were introduced as James, Winter, and Doc. All three
appeared angry and one glanced at his watch.

Mr. White, too, was angry though it did not show in his
demeanor. The unspoken resentment that reached Jo in her
new position trapped between White and James was that Mr.
White felt it's one thing when your son is banging your next
door neighbor; it's quite another when your wife is taking her
pleasure at the same location.

Those familiar with his behavior, including the three men that
they'd just picked up, may not have known the source of his
anger but they knew that was something was up and that his
anger was to be avoided.

At first, the three workers were reluctant to comment openly
about the white bitch their boss had led into the front seat,
the bitch who'd made him late—what if she were his mistress?
But when they saw Mr. White was treating Jo with the same

stony indifference he treated all his employees, they felt free to express their opinions.

For James in the front seat, this meant turning sideways and staring openly at Jo's breasts, as he tried to engage her in increasingly sexual repartee.

For Winter and Doc in the back, it meant freedom to engage in discussion of white women in general, small versus large breasts, the fundamental importance of pussy, and other topics dear to their hearts.

All this only meant that Jo pressed closer to Mr. White in the front seat and that his anger grew correspondingly.

When he stopped the car on the edge of a half-developed lot, she fairly leaped out of the front-seat after him. "Come with me," he said and started toward the half-built house at the rear of the lot. She followed reluctantly and then more easily, after she'd seen that when James tried to follow, Mr. W waved him back.

Mr. White wheeled around at the edge of construction site. "These guys in the car," he said, "I apologize for them. They've obviously not being getting enough lately and having an attractive woman like you this close to them is turning them on."

"I'm scared." Jo said. "Can you take me right home?"

Mr. White was deliberately not reassuring. "We don't want them following you in the house do we? Besides, they're my friends. Come right down to it, I don't really know you. I know them."

"Please," Jo begged. "Just take me back to my car. Or let me off here. I've got my cell phone. I'll phone someone to get me."

"Pull down your panties," he said. Jo remained unmoving, petrified, trying desperately to believe he'd not said what she'd heard him say. He held up a threatening hand. "And hold your skirt up. It's either me bitch, or all of them." He slapped her hands into place, pushed her back against the wall of the building, then bending, tore her panties down below her knees.

She pressed her knees together, placing her hands over her exposed crotch. He was not dissuaded. Reaching forward, he slowly, carefully unbuttoned each of the buttons on her blouse. She reached up to stop him, touched his wrist with her hand. He stepped back bring the hand with him and admired her nakedness. Her remaining hand went to cover her crotch.

The bulge in his pants was huge. A full head taller than she, he stepped forward till his arms were on either side of her and she was pressed against the wall. She could feel his fingers unsnapping her bra, his penis pressed against her fingers.

He slid his cock up and down against her. She was on fire, her lips pressed against the dark skin of his neck, while his fingers played with her nipples.

She wanted to spread her fingers, to touch him, to grasp him with her hand, but held on desperately to what little remained of her self-respect.

When he unzipped his pants, she saw there was no way he could fit its enormity inside her without ripping her open. She thought of Marge's own wide vagina that she'd been made to suck the juice from oh, so many times. The thought made her wet. He brushed his penis against the lips of her vulva. "Please don't," she said, "you'll hurt me."

"Then suck me, white bitch."

She knelt on the ground and proceeded to practice everything she'd learned, hoping against hope as she went through the corncob and the ice-cream cone that he'd come outside her. He did not though, till the instant she took him fully in her mouth. He held her while she gagged and swallowed, the circular breathing technique she'd learned from the film inadequate to hold his enormous load.

As she got to her feet, searching and not finding a handkerchief she could use to wipe his cum from her face and clothes, she noticed her bra was hanging loose, one breast jutting out unloved from her blouse. She started to button her blouse up again. "Leave it," he said, and started down the path toward the car, not looking back, knowing she would follow.

In the car, she could feel the other men's eyes on her. But none spoke; they knew now whose woman she was. Occasionally, Mr. White reached over and squeezed one of her breasts. She turned toward him each time he did so, not wanting the others to see her nakedness. All the other three men could think was how much the white bitch liked it, to think about how they might get a white bitch of their own.

Jo had a dream that night.

In the dream, the three black men had returned and knocked on her door. When she answered, the three had pushed on past her, dragging her behind them down the hallway to her bedroom. There they had taken her, first one at a time, and then in two's and three's, in her mouth, in her vagina, in her behind where no man had ever been.

She awoke shortly after midnight, frustrated, empty and alone. Even her hand could not lull her back to sleep. In the end, she got up and took a shower, directing the spray across her nipples and then against her clitoris. If only, she thought, Noble would come. This time, she would let him inside her, regardless of Marge's warnings.

Anal Sex

The night was warmer than usual. Perhaps, Jo ought to have turned on the air-conditioning. Instead, she tossed and turned all night, sometimes throwing the covers off, sometimes waking chilled to scramble at the foot of the bed until she found the discarded sheets and pull them over her again.

When she woke that morning it was to an erotic dream that involved not Mr. White or her late husband, but Marge's brother, his head between her legs, his tongue probing her vaginal lips. She moaned aloud, realized there was light streaming through the window, and that a very live individual, Noble, crouched between her legs, bringing her unimaginable pleasure.

He stopped just short of completion. She started to sit up, to complain, but he had flipped her over, so now she was face down on her pillow.

Something probed at her rear. His penis? No, it was smoother, smaller, she felt a trickle of liquid, and then all at once the need to go the bathroom was overwhelming.

She rolled away from him, half fell off the edge of the bed and then raced for the bathroom. A moment later, poised on the toilet throne, she had voided her bowels and immediately flushed the toilet.

She stood up and realized that Noble, naked, was standing only a few steps away.

"You don't want to come in," she said. "Let me light a match or open the window." But he had seized her from behind, his hands going to her breasts, and bent her forward over the toilet so that she had to grasp the seat for support.

The next moment she felt a push from behind as though her bowels were working in reverse. He began to thrust himself inside her, first in so far she didn't think it was possible, and then back, the fit between her anus and his cock so tight that her own body jerked back and forth with each of his movements. She could feel him coming inside her, thick white spurts that filled her anus and dripping down her fanny as he popped free.

"Much better," he sighed, "much better." A moment later, he had stepped inside the shower and she could hear the water running. She moved to join him. They kissed, then he was soaping between her legs, first in front, then behind. She felt aroused, could feel the juices gathering at her vaginal lips. He sprang erect again, and turning her so she faced the wall of the shower stall, he pushed inside her from behind a second time, her vagina neglected, the soap on his penis smoothing the way.

This time, one hand left her breast to travel down between her legs, probe gently at her clitoris, and bring her to a climax at the same time as his own frenzied spasms knocked her against the wall.

"Better," she said to please him, though she was still slightly dazed and not quite awake.

"Better."

This time it was she who soaped his penis and cleaned them both.

The Party

As sitting was somewhat uncomfortable, Jo decided to work in the garden that morning. Crouching also wasn't without its discomfort so Jo settled on trimming her hedges and pruning her fruit trees, both of which could be done while standing upright.

She had almost but not quite completed a circuit of the backyard when a ringing telephone summoned her inside.

The call came from Marge who had phoned to tell her there would be an impromptu party at her home that evening. "It will be somewhat on the formal side. Is this enough notice?"

The party was formal, and Jo was not certain that the light sundress she'd worn would prove adequate. In contrast to the last party she'd attended at Marge's, this one was held indoors and the procession of meats from an outdoor barbeque were replaced by a procession of waiters bearing hors d'ouevre from the caterers in the White's kitchen.

The other main difference from the previous party and indeed from all the social gatherings she'd attended at Marge's was that there were quite a few Caucasians present besides her, business associates of Mr. Whites, she surmised.

Though she was not the only white, still, people seemed to be staring at her, not directly, but stolen glances, quickly turning away whenever she looked back.

All about the room, the guests stood in little groups. Only she was alone.

She wished Noble would come over if only to have a quick reassuring few words with her. She could see him across the room, in the midst of a circle of adults with whom one by one he was shaking hands.

"Seat?" An older gentleman, a "wool" as the other blacks would call him, had risen from the sofa and was offering her his place.

"No, thank you," she replied, worried that she might have appeared discourteous. Regardless, he would not be sitting down that evening. And I'll probably have to sleep on my side, she thought.

Velma came slinking toward her then, glass in hand; as always, her false bosoms preceded her at some distance. Her form-fitting dress came with a choke collar. Judged by its label, it was expensive. Still, when draped over Velma any dress looked cheap.

"Enjoying yourself," Velma asked, slipping an arm around Jo's waist. She obviously didn't expect an answer and Jo didn't offer her one.

"Want to sit down and have a girl talk?"

About what? "Not this evening." Jo had no intention of sitting down, much less sitting to talk with someone she despised.

The hand around Jo's waist slipped down and patted Jo firmly on her bottom. "Ouch," Jo exclaimed involuntarily.

"Does that hurt?"

"Velma behave." said Marge, appearing just in time to deflect Velma's unwanted attention. "Jo may be feeling just a little sore this evening."

"Still, I'll bet she likes the feeling it gives her."

Jo balled her fists. Her sole desire at that moment was to rip the choke collar from around Velma's throat and take her scrawny neck along with it. But Velma and Marge had already moved away.

Had anyone noticed the quarrel? Had anyone heard what the two women had said? Once again, she could tell that people were looking at her and then quickly looking away when she looked back. Did they all know what had happened?

When she saw a recent arrival, a stout black man, almost as solidly built and as tall as Mr. White, shake Noble's hand, she realized that of course they did. This was a party to celebrate Noble's becoming a man. And she was there, his conquest, living proof of his manhood.

She felt like screaming, "Yes, but he never fucked me where I want to be fucked." But, of course, she didn't.

The French Maid

Noble's coming of age party was to be the least of Jo's degradations at the White's hands. Invited to tea the following week, Marge told her not to worry about what to wear. Once, Jo would have spent an hour dressing before going to one of Marge's teas, trying on and discarding half a dozen outfits. This time, Marge ordered her to put on a black maid's outfit and serve the other guests. The dress was far too small. Its deeply scooped neck placed both her small breasts on display, so that they constantly threatened to break loose if she bent over too far while serving tea. And Marge's guests made sure that she was constantly bending.

The abbreviated skirt that came with the maid's outfit barely covered her white panties and when she bent forward the pink flesh of her buttocks was immediately revealed. More than one woman at Marge's table put their hand up Jo's skirt that day.

Once, Marge made her sit in her lap while the other guests looked on. Slowly, dreamily, as if not quite aware of what she was doing, she plucked out each of Jo's small breasts from the scooped neckline, slowly examined them, gently caressing each nipple before she placed them back inside the blouse again.

Every guest there knew she was now Marge's plaything. In fact, Millie and Velma and two other black women whose names Jo did not know came with them when Marge led her back into the bedroom.

Marge sat at her dressing table, watching in the mirror as Jo was made to undress her. Carefully, Jo undid, and then hung up Marge's gown. She unsnapped Marge's girdle and then her brassiere, Marge giving a sigh of relief as her breasts broke free. Only then, did she turn around to face Jo.

They could hear sounds from the other room, the other guests chattering away as they cleared the dishes from the table.

"Shall I shut the door?" Jo asked.

"On your knees bitch." was Marge's only reply.

Jo got down on her knees before Marge, slipped Marge's panties from around her ample thighs as instructed, then bent to bury her head in her mistresses' pussy.

Were the other women watching as she did this?

Marge opened her thighs. "You can shut the door now child."

When Jo returned—the other women had been watching—Marge led her to the bed and covering Jo's slight body with her own, proceeded use her mouth and hands to bring Jo to orgasm after orgasm before declaring herself satisfied with Jo's attentions.

As one by one the other women left the room, Jo raised herself up on one elbow.

"Stay," Marge ordered as she left, and closed the bedroom door behind her.

Millie's Place.

After almost all the guests had left, Marge returned and told Jo she would be spending the night at Millie's.

"Millie liked what she saw. She wants to spend time with you."

Jo knew better than to protest. Nothing would be gained by it.

Milly's interest in Jo had begun innocently enough. Like more than one woman at the party, though much older than the majority, she had pulled Jo in her maid's uniform into her lap, played with Jo's breasts and then put her hand up Jo's skirt.

But her hand had stayed there longer than the others, and her fingers had stroked Jo so gently that when Jo came she had cradled Millie's head in her hands and kissed her over and over.

In the car, they were no sooner free of the White's driveway, then Millie had her lie down across the front seat and put her head in Millie's lap. For a while, Mille had contented herself cupping Jo's breasts and caressing her nipples. Then, one hand on the steering wheel, she had pulled her dress up almost to her waist and welcomed Jo's mouth between her legs.

When they parked finally in Millie's driveway, she held Jo's head between her thighs for a final moment, and gave a long satisfied sigh before pulling free and smoothing down her dress.

"You could be mine," she said. But before she could say more, two young boys who couldn't have mean more than ten or eleven, Millie's grandchildren, were pounding on the car doors.

Millie gave each of them a hug and then introduced them to Jo with whom they shook hands solemnly.

Inside the house, cries of "cake, grandma" could be heard, but the children were told they would first have to eat supper. Jo offered to help fix the meal, but was told it was her task to keep the boys occupied. This did not prove difficult, as one by one the boys brought a procession of toys for Jo to admire, until a call to the dinner table ended their show.

The older of the two boys said grace, and all pitched in to an ample meal that included okra, ribs, and buttermilk biscuits, the boys occasionally being instructed on the use of "please," and "thank you." Only after cake had been served along with a second glass of milk for each boy, did Jo realize one of the other reasons why she had been invited to spend the night at Millie's.

After the boys had cleared the table, the family retired to the living room, where Millie had them all sit side by side on the long sofa. She asked Jo to stand. Jo complied, though she felt awkward and embarrassed at being the center of attention.

"Now lift your skirt dear."

Jo froze, trying not to believing she'd heard what she'd heard Millie say. Millie did her best to reassure Jo, as if the request and Jo's need to follow through on it were quite normal at her house. "The boys are at an age don't you see when they need to be aware of the differences between men and women."

Finally, when Jo still did not move, Millie rose and standing just behind her, lifted her skirt so the boys could see. Of course, as Jo was still wearing her French Maid outfit, absent panties or bra, there wasn't much they couldn't.

"She's got hair," one said.

"Just the way you've got hair there, now. I told you it was natural as you grow older."

"She doesn't have a you know."

"It's called a penis, dear. Say penis."

The boys repeated the word several times.

Jo turned beet red as Millie explained that Jo being a girl had a vagina. Perhaps, she would not have blushed had not Millie pointed to it, touching Jo's labia with her finger.

The boys also got to see Jo's breasts, which were taken one at a time from Jo's low-cut halter-top and held out for inspection. They learned the words "breast," "aureole," and "nipple" after which they were told they were to put on their pajamas and get ready for bed.

"Story," one hollered.

"Pajamas first," was the firm reply.

"It's quite late, dear," Millie said to Jo, "I'm quite tired, also. I think its time we both went to sleep."

To Jo's surprise, she would sleep in her own bedroom rather than with Millie and was offered a see-though nightgown to take to bed with her to wear in place of the maid's outfit.

She had taken a bath and was in bed in the night gown Millie had given her, when the bedroom door opened and Millie came in followed by her two rambunctious grand children.

"They wants you to read them a story," Millie said, and handed her a book with large print and pictures.

The two children slipped into bed beside her one on each side and she began to read, though it seemed odd this would be necessary at their age. The book, too, seemed aimed at much younger children, not ones so clearly poised on the brink of adolescence.

After Millie had left the room, shutting the door behind her, the two grandchildren, till then as quiet as mice, suddenly came alive. Jo tried to concentrate on the book she was reading, something about a mouse that had both a cat and dog for friends, but this was almost impossible while the pair were busy exploring the differences between men and women. Several times she had to bat their hands away from her newly discovered vagina. She let them explore her breasts though and when each took a nipple in their mouth and began to suck, she thought it best to leave them alone as long as they were quiet and continued to read, noting that one by one the children dropped off to sleep.

Finally, she shut the book, turned off the light and tried to go to sleep herself.

It was difficult. She thought about the two boys sleeping next to her. Occasionally, one would flail about in his sleep, and arm or a hand would come to rest against her. By accident? Or on purpose? The sexual intent she read into their movements lay entirely in her own mind.

She wondered if they were at all close to sexual maturity, if she might wake during the middle of the night to find one or the other inside her. She thought of reaching down and touching the older one's penis to see if it would come erect.

These thoughts kept her awake for some time. Millie too had to be asleep for she could no longer hear movement anywhere in the house, just the regular tick-tock of the grandfather clock in the parlor, the occasional drip from a half-closed tap, the sound of a refrigerator turning on and then off, and then, Jo too was asleep.

In the early morning, when it was still quite dark, Jo felt a tap on her shoulder, and heard Millie, say "shh." Millie helped her slip out the bottom of the bed so that she wouldn't wake the boys and then led her down the hall to her own bedroom. There, Jo experienced the orgasm she had longed for earlier, Millie being a far more gifted lover than Marge would ever be, before being led back down the hall again, where once more she crept beneath the covers, pulled the sheet up so that it covered both her and the boys and fell into a dreamless sleep.

In the morning, she discovered that the two boys could get erections, for both had begun to rub themselves against her. She turned away irritably only to realize that once she was on her side, each of them could then fit themselves between her thighs, the one with his nose pressed against her back, the other taking her nipple in his mouth.

Their movements were frantic unfocused, ending with both of them spraying her with their cum simultaneously, after which they jumped out of bed and ran down the hall, screaming, "grandma, grandma, we cum against the lady."

Roland's Return

Marge phoned shortly after Noble left for school that morning, asking Jo if she'd like to come over, as if she had a choice any longer. As always Marge led her immediately into the bedroom, but this morning, sex was not what Marge had in mind.

"I really just need to talk. Roland's coming."

"Roland? Your older boy?"

"Yes. I miss him so. He comes and goes, has been that way since he was sixteen.

"Joined the Marines. I'm so proud. But he never writes. Then comes a phone call out of the blue, "I'm coming home, mom.""

"Do you want to?" Mrs. White asked, changing the subject abruptly. She lay back against the pillows, one huge black breast becoming visible in the opening of her housecoat.

Jo shook her head. "I don't think so. I told you, I don't think it's right."

"I understand. Well, anyway Roland's coming, Roland's coming home."

Amazingly Marge got up then and with Jo trailing behind her walked into the living room, there to snap on the TV and then ignoring it, to turn on the vacuum, sweeping an already immaculate carpet, dusting surfaces that did not require dusting.

Forgotten and ignored, Jo let herself out.

Jo didn't actually see Roland's arrival that day; she'd been out showing prospective clients homes in the new development, but she knew he had returned.

No calls from the White home that evening. Even Noble failed to put in an appearance. It was family time at the Whites.

Frustrated, but grateful, that her life seemed to have returned to normal, Jo watched TV that evening, took a long hot bath, trimmed her bangs, shaved her legs. Me time. She lay down, tossed about restlessly, then got up and took a cold shower. This time when she went to bed she fell instantly asleep.

A click told her that the French doors that led into her bedroom from the outside had been forced once again. But it was not Noble who stood there that morning. The young man who stood in the doorway was taller, fuller in the chest, and somehow more dignified. Roland.

His penis was longer, slimmer than Nobles and slid easily between the open lips of her pussy as he clasped her from behind his hands caressing and kneading her breasts.

Just as Jo felt him on the verge of coming, he had withdrawn, spun her around in bed, and brought her mouth to his waiting member. She tried to move her head, but it was held rigid between his two strong hands. She opened, and then choked as he forced his long organ deep inside. The pressure on her head eased. Noble's strong hands moved to her breasts and began to stroke her nipples. Grateful, she began to suck long and lovingly on his penis tasting the strange mixture of her own juices mixed with his as she willed him to come.

But again, just when it seemed inevitable that he would come inside her mouth, he withdrew, spun her around again, and flipped her over, so that he pressed down on her shoulders. He fucked long and deep inside her pussy from behind, stroke after long stroke, then shorter, faster. She came again and again, willing him deep inside her.

When he had come in turn, he remained on the bed beside her, his arms around her, the two of them cupped like spoons.

Had they slept? When she woke, she was on her stomach again, with him on top his penis probing her ass. Not there, she wanted to shout, but her head was pressed against the pillows barely allowing her to breathe. She felt a push inside her, felt she was loosing control. His slim hand reached beneath her body, probed till it contacted her clitoris, flicked it lightly, and then withdrew so that his fingers were barely touching. She began to move her own body, straining to make contact with his finger, ignoring the jarring probing of his member as it tunneled inside her.

She slept then, his cum on her lips, in her vagina, up her ass. When she woke he was gone.

Afternoon came before she woke a second time. She had missed all her morning appointments. She had another client, from out of town, due in several hours but thought there's time to go next door first and see if he wants me.

She chose a long wool dress that she had not worn in some time. Too warm for the present weather perhaps, but she was only going next door. The dress revealed every curve of her body. Her husband has often urged her to wear it when they went out together. "Drives other men crazy," he'd said, "Because they know I'm getting it and their not."

When she stepped through the hedge that separated their two properties, she found Marge standing in her driveway. She looked shaken. "He's gone," she said. "I wanted you to meet him. But he jus' up and went. Tha's his way. I fixed a big breakfast for him. Didn't eat it."

Jo thought, I know where he got his breakfast.

"Child give me a hug," Marge begged.

Jo did. And when Marge asked her to come inside with her, Jo went unprotesting.

Camping Trip

"We'd like you to come on a camping trip with us," Marge opened their phone conversation one morning.

"Not to worry, we won't be sleeping outdoors or anything, we'll be staying in a motel. But there will be hiking and picnics, maybe a boat ride."

Jo said yes; she was no longer sure how to say no to Marge.

The White's Lincoln town car was spacious enough, though she didn't really fancy sitting in the back seat between Noble and a second boy, a strange one, a nephew of Marge's apparently, who wore glasses, stuttered, and wouldn't look Jo in the eye.

She only wished Noble was half as shy and several times had to push his hands away. "Wait till we're in private," she whispered.

"Ain't nevr goin' t'be. I didn't ask to go camping. Or to bring this fool along."

Despite what he just had said about his still unnamed cousin, Noble chose to sit next to him after their first rest stop, and the two played some device, which beeped and lit up as its various keys were pressed. Strangely, Jo felt neglected rather than relieved.

Their motel was perched on the edge of a state park, and despite its name, Campground Motel, there was nothing rustic about it. The windows of the second floor room that she shared with Marge—"Girls, in one room, boys in the other."— looked out over a thick woods. The men, she was assured, had themselves a view of the lake.

Both rooms were equipped with a small refrigerator, microwave over, and a coffee maker. But when suppertime came, they moved to a picnic ground adjoining the hotel where Mr. White prepared steaks for the adults and hamburgers for the boys.

Only after they'd changed into their nightclothes, did Marge ask if Jo would mind spending a half hour or so in the boy's room, so Marge could have some time alone with her husband.

Instead of going immediately to sleep as she'd hoped, Jo spent the next half hour in her robe sitting up with the boys as they watched television cross-legged on the bed.

Noble's hand kept creeping up her leg of course. When she'd pushed it away for the third or fourth time, he moved to the head of the bed next to her and began to massage her breast.

"Your cousin," Jo hissed.

"I fix that." Noble turned off the light and in the next moment had used the remote to turn off the TV.

"Hey, I was watching that."

"We going to sleep now." Noble replied and the next moment had opened her robe and was making himself at home at her breast.

She was surprised but not entirely displeased, when the cousin took his place on her remaining bosom.

Once the TV was off, the sounds carried through the open windows and the thin motel walls made it obvious how Marge and her husband were spending the time together. The half hour Marge had spoken of was long since over but they showed no signs of stopping.

Meanwhile, Noble's hands were everywhere, while the cousin's pajamas as well as Noble's had disappeared.

"I'm going to leave," Jo threatened. A cock presented itself near her open mouth. Was it Noble's? The cousins? She pushed it away or tried to; it wasn't Noble's. Then it was Noble who was eagerly licking at her labia, trying for but not quite finding her clitoris. Her hot spot he called it. "I's trying to find your hot spot."

He found her hotspot and when he pushed himself inside her, she gave up pushing the cousin's penis away and took it in her mouth. The pair came quickly and not very satisfyingly inside her.

Was Marge never going to return? Were those snores she could now hear coming from the adjoining room?

But the pair of boys made up for the quickness with which they'd come with the quickness that they came erect again. Noble entered her a second time. Or was it the cousin? They took turns, moving more slowly and taking longer each time they were inside her. And finally she, too, was aroused and spasming, adding her cum to theirs.

In the early morning hours, she asked them to stop, presenting her hands, her mouth, and then her anus in turn to get relief for her by now aching cunt.

The Picnic in the Woods

A knock on the door early the next morning, announced that they would all be going down to the motel restaurant for breakfast.

The first thing her eyes lit upon was the bent head of the cousin who was once again wearing his glasses. Once again he would not meet her eye and kept his gaze steadfast on the floor, though he must have seen all there was of her in the night before if only in the half-light that streamed through the window.

She still remembered the pair's final sandwich-like embrace, one from the front, one from her rear, though she could not remember which of the two boys had entered her from the front and which from behind.

Both ends ached though. Still, she felt light and gay, fully relaxed, as they tripped down the motel stairs together.

"Pretty noisy up there last night," Mr. White said as the three of them joined the couple at their table. Jo realized, as she should have long before, that last night, too, had been a planned part of the camping trip.

She was able to order, but thereafter, the boys were determined to keep her hands busy in their laps. Fortunately, once the food arrived, they took turns feeding her, using her own utensils, so that she didn't go without breakfast.

Neither of the older Whites remarked on the oddity of it all. They merely grinned at each other, for they too seemed relaxed and happy and gay.

"Can we go for a hike now?" the boys, or, at least, Noble asked after breakfast.

"First, we'll pack the car," Mr. White replied. "That way we won't have to rush back afterward."

Despite, Mr. White's admonishment to stay on the trail, one after the other of the boys would lead her off on a side expedition, the cousin merely taking Jo's hand to communicate his desire. Once out of sight of the others, the boys were eager to mount her and she would have to explain that she was still sore and it would not be possible.

She began to wonder if she could not get someone to help her satisfy the steadily increasing desires of the White family. Short little Linda from across the street perhaps. What she lacked in stature, she made up for with the size of her breasts. Linda was married, and as far as Jo knew had never been unfaithful, but her husband was on the road a lot, and who knew perhaps she could be persuaded, as Joanne had, to help out.

There was Andrea. Andrea didn't know that Jo knew, but she did. Andrea's garage door having gone up one day, while Andrea was still in the act of stuffing her blouse back in her skirt, and the young man, the very young man who was with her had yet to pull up his pants. Still, that young man had been white. Would Andrea be willing to change her luck?

By this time in her thoughts, Noble or his cousin would have unzipped or pulled down their pants completely and expect Joanne to go to work.

When she seemed reluctant, they would take her hand and pull her down to them, so half standing and half crouching, she found it easier to go down on her knees and do exactly as the boys requested.

She was grateful when Marge took her turn with her, as no explanations regarding Jo's sore pussy would be necessary. Still, she began to long for the plentiful me time she'd had as a widow before the Whites moved in.

Mr. White was a surprisingly gentle lover that day. He kissed Joanne all over her body, caressing her breasts and separating her thighs to suck at her overflowing cunt, before he again attempted to insert himself. "Got to have Marge here, so I can do you both at once," he snarled when he realized insertion of so large an object in so small an opening would be impossible, "suck you, fuck her." But Marge was with the boys, so again Joanne found herself on her knees trying to swallow more cum than she'd believed could ever spring forth from one man.

The smell of pines was everywhere. Birds hopped about in the underbrush and woodpeckers could be heard, though always just ahead or behind them on the trail. After lunch, they bathed in the lake, the older Whites in bathing suits they'd recently purchased, the boys and Joanne naked in the suits nature alone had provided.

As Mr. White led Jo into the woods for the second time that day, he realized Marge has been right all along. His way had only acquired a woman for his oldest son; her way yielded a sex slave that could be used by the entire family.

Jay Again

I wonder if Joanne ever did get Linda or Adriana to help her? Ask anyone on the block and they'll tell you Linda is both model housewife and ideal mother. Few can resist looking on through their windows whenever she wheels a pram up and down the block. They'll step out for a moment or stop watering their lawn in order to chuck her child under its tiny chin. With a second child to take care of, one only a few months old now, she hardly ever leaves the neighborhood, except once a week, when her mother, an equally buxom, but far too stout woman comes over to baby-sit.

But I'll let you read her story for yourself. I'll be kinda busy this afternoon as Joanne's coming over. Lovely girl. I just hate that half the money I give her, including the tip, will go to that obnoxious little colored boy.

Phillip Good 844 words

205 W. Utica Ave.

Huntington Beach CA 92648

jcuzse@yahoo.com

LINDA

No doubt about it, Linda was cute as a button.Her small, delicate features had brought this comment from passing strangers even when she was a child.

Adolescence had been kind to her. Her teeth required no braces; her skin no special acne fighting creams.

Her breasts, once apples, became first small cantaloupes, and then, as her husband described them when she was pregnant with their second child, cannon balls.

She'd met her husband when she was in the eleventh grade and he was in the twelfth. He was incredibly handsome. She'd always been sensitive about her height and his six feet two inches promised that daughters, if they had them, would be taller than she.

They'd dated for three years and then married when she found she was pregnant with Jason. Fortunately, he hadn't needed to finish college.

He'd been promoted rapidly at P&G and by the time April, their second child, arrived, he was already an area manager.

Unfortunately, this also meant he had to be on the road much of the time. A third child would have to be delayed, she confided to her mother. And with him away and Jason and April both so active, she could use the occasional helping hand.

So every Wednesday afternoon, her mother came to baby-sit, leaving Linda free to spend the afternoon in an air-conditioned movie theater pretending she had every bit as active and exciting a life as the characters on the screen.

She was already swept up in the action that afternoon when the two men sat down on either side of her. She would have ignored them indefinitely had not the one stuck a knife into her ribs and informed her in a harsh whisper that she was to remain silent and not move.

First the knife cut through her bra straps, though he might easily have undone them, sparing her the need for an equally expensive replacement. The cannon balls leaped forth.

Hands reached out from either side to explore their round contours and stroke her nipples. She resolved to continue to watch the movie regardless, and to try to forget the two men were there.

This became increasingly difficult to do, particularly after her blouse was unbuttoned and each of the men took one of her nipples in his mouth.

Oh well, when April woke up that afternoon, she would have to make do with one of the stored bottles that Linda saved in case she ever ran dry, not that she ever had.

Hands began to stoke her thighs and she pressed them tightly together. She was a good girl after all.

When a hand pressed on the back of her neck and tilted her forward so that she faced the one man's lap, she realized that might not be possible that afternoon.

Though she had sucked only one's man's cock since her last year of high school, she had lost none of her skills in this area and the operation was soon completed with a loss of only a few lines of the film's dialog.

The second man wanted his turn. She pointed to her throat. He understood immediately and shared his soft drink with her. Once her mouth was rinsed, to show her gratitude, she attacked his member with equal fervor.

Somewhere, amid all this activity, her panties had been removed or ripped from her and the first man's fingers were actively at work inside her cunt. She moaned.

"We'd best go outside," the second man whispered. "Don't want to disturb these people."

She followed them, not unwillingly, up the aisle out into the bright sunlight and across the mall parking lot to the rear of their panel truck.

A worn mattress covered its metal floor. They boosted her up into the truck, and then shut the door behind them from inside.

A mustached face came down between her legs while the other man again offered his penis for an appetizer. She was less successful in bringing him to a climax this time, for she found the first man's toying with her clitoris distracting. When the latter lifted his head from between her legs, it allowed her to regain her concentration, but a moment later, he had pushed his cock inside her. Forgetting the first man completely, though his dripping cock hung inches from her mouth, she abandoned herself completely to the second's ministrations. Alas, he came too quickly, far quicker than could be satisfying. But then moustache took the other's place. He moved slowly, carefully inside her, taking great pleasure from each of her moans, from the frantic movements of her hips. Finally, she gave a little scream, and the three came together, the first man's cum showering on her from above.

For several moments, the threesome lay like puppies cuddled next to their dam, exhausted but happy. Then Linda looked at her watch. "Oh my goodness," she said, sitting up on the mattress and pushing the men aside. "I have to go." She wiped her face with a towel.

"Next Wednesday?" she suggested as she slipped out of the truck and onto the pavement.

Jay

Uh, oh, who's that I see sneaking out of Adriana's garage? A happily married woman, especially one with two teen-age children, can't afford to fool around unless whoever she's fooling around with stays well clear of where she lives. This next story is about the time she unthinkingly broke the rule.

Adrianna

When she first saw the young man, Adrianna Barnes was on her way home from a most unsatisfactory shopping trip.

Why was it so hard to find a bra the right size only to discover the next time you went shopping that the model you'd chosen had been discontinued?

The young man stood fidgeting at a bus stop, standing first on one leg, than the other, shivering in the cold. Eighteen or nineteen, he moved awkwardly as if he'd just received a new body and hadn't got used to driving around in it yet.

If it hadn't been for the rain and the fact that she'd had to stop for the light anyway she would never have given him a lift.

"Get in," she said. His only reply was a furtive smile but he did get in the car. She looked him over carefully, not entirely thrilled by what she saw. She supposed his mother might love him but didn't suppose too many other women would care for this gawky teenager.

Tall as a tree, perhaps, but more of a willow than an oak. Not much for conversation. Not even a "Thanks for getting me in out of the rain."

In fact, the first time he spoke was when he pointed to the left and said, "you turn here."

The new road took them by a park on the right, which gave her an idea. Perhaps, she might have a bit of fun with him. Geek.

But at the place where he indicated to her he should get out, a crowd of teenagers stood shooting hoops.

"Is there somewhere quieter?" she asked.

"On the other side of the park, but I live . . ."

She ignored what he was about to say next, made a quick right turn at the foot of the block and then a second right turn a moment or so later. An unbroken stand of trees lined the park's far side; quieter all right. Again without consulting him, she pulled off the road into a shallow parking area, split in the middle by a single path leading deeper into the trees.

She undid her safety belt then and turned in her seat to face him.

"All right, show me."

The boy looked confused, which, of course was what she wanted.

"Unzip, take it out, show me. Your manhood, stupid.

"Do I have to do it for you?" she added when the boy sat frozen in place. "Afraid? What's your name?

"Jason."

"Just do it Jason. Do what I say."

Jason unzipped, his face registering a thousand kinds of panic, but nothing protruded.

"That's all there is?"

"I'm scared."

"Maybe if I touched it." The boy flinched when she reached out.

"Stroke it," she ordered, "Make it large, larger anyway."

The boy fiddled with himself for a few seconds but nothing of importance materialized. Geek.

She slid across the seat and gripped him by the shoulders. "Stay still." The next moment she leaned down and kissed the tip of his flaccid member. The result was instantaneous. His penis rose from his pants like a mushroom opening to the rain, only the result, Adrianna thought, was far more impressive.

For a skinny kid, he had a remarkably thick and large penis. The sort that might be well worth sucking. She leaned down once more to kiss the tip, when without warning he ejaculated a thick heavy cream that not only splashed across her face and blouse but got into her hair and onto the dashboard.

"Don't you have any self control!" she screamed as her tongue licked at her cum-coated lips. "Get out of my car!"

"But I live . . ." he began.

"Get out."

Jason opened the door and slid outside to the ground. The rain was now falling in earnest.

"And do up your pants!"

Geek.

She passed the boy at the bus stop once more the following week but drove on by. What a waste of time he had been.

The incident had been amusing at least, that is, once she'd cleaned up the mess. Luckily, she'd glanced in the mirror a second time before going into her home as a few drops of cum still clung to her hair. He had such a beautiful cock, though. On impulse, she made a U-turn and sped back to where he still stood waiting by the roadside.

"Get in," she said.

"I masturbated this morning," he told her proudly as he slipped into the car.

"What!"

"I won't come as quickly."

"Better not." She smiled as she said it; this might be fun after all.

They returned to the same place she had parked the day before. She couldn't help notice on the drive that there was already a little tent formed in his pants. That cock of his had been so enormous, so desirable.

As the car rolled to a stop, they undid their safety belts almost simultaneously. He turned toward her and unzipped in the same motion, his penis reaching out just waiting to be sucked.

But best go slow. "Do you have any math homework, today?" she asked.

"Math homework?" he repeated.

"I want you to think about your homework, concentrate on it as I get to work."

She planned to give the little retard an experience he would never forget, would eat his heart out longing to repeat. Still, he did have such a beautiful penis, its outside soft as velvet.

She began with little bites along the shaft, then licked her way to the top. When he moaned once, she whispered, "Math," and then went back to work.

First the bites, then the licks as if the head of his penis were an ice cream cone.From time to time, she would fit the head of his shaft into her mouth, give it a quick suck, then reach out and pinch his thigh to ensure he would not come too soon.

Still, inevitably, Jason would and must climax. At the moment when her mouth was engorging not only the head of his penis but as much of his shaft as her mouth and throat would hold, she felt his hips rising. She tried to raise her head own head to escape, but his hand was on the back of her neck, pressing down, keeping her head in place. Damn it, she should have told him to keep his hands to himself.

In an instant, her mouth and throat filled with the creamy liquid. She swallowed as much as she could but, inevitably, it spilled out the sides of her mouth, down her cheeks and onto her dress.

"You're too much for me," she panted happily a few seconds later, and began trying to mop up with her handkerchief. Perhaps, she ought to keep a towel in her car, not that she planned to do anything like this ever again.

He started to slip out the door as he had the day before, but she stopped him. "I'll drive you home," she said.

"Gosh thanks, Mrs. Barnes."

How did he know her name! "Do I know you?" she asked, her voice not as calm as she would have liked.

'Don't you remember? I was on your son's team."

"His team?" she repeated. Now who was this retard?

"His soccer team."

Soccer? That had been what, four or five years ago. Jason would have been the little towhead, a year younger than the others, who was never quite where he was supposed to be on the field.

And she had just given him a first class blowjob.

"You were always the best, Mrs. Barnes." he said.

The next day she began to worry. If he knew her name, did he not also know where she lived? Would he expect to see her again?

The answer to her questions came that afternoon when he telephoned. "Can I see you today? Could we meet in the park this afternoon?"

"I don't think so. No, that would not be a good idea. Besides, I have company this afternoon. And, I'll probably be busy most of this week."

"You're all alone in the house," he interrupted. "You don't have company."

Alone? How could he possibly know that? "Where are you?" She carried the telephone to the window and peered out. Could that be him in the gray automobile?

"Just outside. I borrowed my mom's car. Can I come in?"

"No! My husband will be home any minute. Look, you can't park outside my house. You've got to go away."

"Could I come in? Just for a minute? I could park in your garage."

What if the neighbors saw him? Still, the fastest way to get rid of him would be to give him a quick blow job and then send him on his way. She'd figure out how to get rid of him permanently later.

"I'll open the garage door," she said and started toward the garage, the phone card trailing behind her. The door had gone up before she realized she was wearing only a housecoat. Well, it wouldn't matter. He'd be on his way soon enough.

The minute his card was inside the garage, she lowered the door again. The less the neighbors saw the better. He had slid over into the passenger seat, unzipped and spread his legs by the time she reached the car. His penis stood wagging before her like an upside down pendulum.

"Give me some room," she said and crawled into the car to kneel below the dashboard.

She reached out a hand, wondering if he would shy away, but, no, he seemed to be expecting it. He reached out his own hand at the same time and touched one of her breasts through the opening in the house coat. "You have wonderful breasts," he said, "You always did. You were the best stacked team mother. We all thought so. Can I suck them?"

Who do you think you are, my lover? Aloud, she said, " No you cannot. Not today. There isn't time. You can hold on to them though, it will help you come quickly." And shoving his cock into her mouth she began to suck on it as hard and fast as she could, pulling it in and out of her mouth at the same time.

But there was no immediate result.

What was the matter with him? Why hadn't he come? Was he still thinking about math? She reached down with her long fingernails and stroked his scrotum at the same time as she slid her mouth slowly down and around the full length of his penis. He came with a gush, her mouth and throat filling with a thick cream as before.

Again she swallowed. Again there was too much for her throat to hold, and cum dripped down her chin and onto her housecoat, falling too on her speckled breasts.

They heard a door slam inside the house at that moment. Followed by footsteps that led into the kitchen only a few feet away. She gripped her housecoat tightly. Her other hand, surprisingly, still held his penis.

"It's my son," she whispered. "What if he finds us?" But the noises in the kitchen soon subsided and they could hear feet going up the stairs.

"He must have gone up to his room." Jason said.

"You've got to go."

"Let me help you first." He reached out to try to wipe the cum from her face, but she shied away. "Go, just go."

Later, as he sailed along in the family Oldsmobile, Jason realized how very fortunate he was. Today he'd held her breast and got a look at her snatch. Next time, he would give her a good sucking, both the left and the right titties, and maybe even give her a finger job. And after that, who knew? All the way for sure. He fairly bounced up and down in the driver's seat with excitement.

Jay

Liz, Liz. What would I do without her once a week visits?
Probably, I'd throw tennis balls at the adjoining house until
Linda came over to satisfy my needs. Liz is pricey, Linda does
it purely for the sex, but Liz is well worth the money.

Liz was a good girl when she and her husband started out
together, a straight arrow. If her husband had paid more
attention to her and less to his job, perhaps things would not
have turned out the way they did. Not that I'm unhappy with
the way things turned out; not at all.

Liz

She'd no sooner opened the door to her apartment then a knife was held to her throat.

"Don't scream."

When the pressure on her throat was eased, she asked, "What do you want? We don't have much money."

"I don't want money." She felt the prick of the knife now in her lower back. "Walk forward slowly. Slowly! One step at a time. Now turn around."

When she turned around, the glare from the side window was in her eyes, and the figure at the front door was hidden in shadow.

"Take off your clothes."

Her hand clutched at her throat in response, then stopped, frozen.

The man made a threatening gesture. "Unbutton your blouse."

This time, she hastened to comply, fumbling with the buttons till finally the blouse opened exposing her bra and her bare midriff.

"I see you use a front loader." He chuckled. "Now, unsnap it."

She unsnapped her bra and her breasts fell free. A natural C, her breasts looked smaller perhaps because her nipples were so large. "Now, turn around."

She felt mildly irritated; didn't he like her bosoms? Most men did. Her husband was crazy about them. She turned as directed; then his arms were around her, a breast in each of his hands, his fingers playing with her nipples, barely grazing them, then stroking, then a mere whisper of a touch.

Her mind remembered a half-completed Karate lesson, strike down along his leg with the heel, then smash his instep, but he had the knife and besides, she felt limp all over. Her first orgasm had come this same way, by herself in the bathtub, her fingers grazing her nipples, stroking them just as he was doing now.

When he unbuttoned her skirt and let it fall to the floor, she made no attempt to resist.

The room was so silent; the only sound her rapid breathing.

He removed his fingers. "No," she said, unable to contain herself, startled by the sound of her own voice.

His hand pressed down on her back, and she bent forward; his penis entered her vagina at the same time and she came instantly. Then he was working it back and forth inside her as if he had all the time in the world. Each stroke brought her closer and closer to a second climax.

"Fuck me, fuck me," she shouted as if he needed encouragement. The strokes grew wilder. Once he slipped out and she reached down and thrust him back in again. When she came for the third time, he came too wet and sticky.

The hands came down from her breasts, one to her vagina where the heel of his palm just barely grazed her clitoris, and one to slip her panties down over her firm buttocks.

The hand at her vagina was replaced by a finger, then two fingers, then three, making only light touches, each time opening her wider and wider. The other hand was at her breast again.

"Don't turn around," he warned.

"I've got to sit down."

Still behind her, his hand on her breast, he guided her to a kitchen chair. When she sat down exhausted, he remained behind the chair until he had tied a dishtowel around her eyes as if they were about to play a game of blind man's buff.

The refrigerator door opened, then closed. He obviously had found something he liked because she could hear the sound of chewing, followed by the sound of a liquid being poured into a glass. She started when she suddenly felt a drop of moisture on her nipple; his mouth followed. "Milk from the source," he said.

"We haven't had a child yet," she mumbled as if this were somehow important. First one nipple, than the other received his attention and she was halfway to a second, no a third orgasm. Unconsciously, she reached down and cradled his head in her hands as if he were her husband and lover rather than some dreadful man who had broken into their apartment. When he eased her up out of the chair and sat down on it himself, she spread her legs immediately at his touch and sat down on his lap facing him. Their hands met as they both tried to guide him quickly inside her.

He had taken her nipple into his mouth again, through there was no milk this time unless his previous efforts had somehow stimulated production. She braced herself, hands on his shoulders and began to move slowly up and down, seeking to find just the right angle, just the right rhythm.

"You're doing all the work," he said, releasing her nipple for the moment. She had no breath with which to reply. She was so close to coming and then she was convulsing, her vagina closing down around his penis, bringing him deeper into her.

"Wow," he said.

When her orgasm had subsided he began to move and to move her, the long strokes accompanied by little bites on her breasts and shoulders. Then his hips were thrusting upward out of control and once again, they came together.

He lifted her away from him finally and staggered to his feet. "I could use that dish towel," he said. "No, don't take it off."

He ran the water in the sink; he'd found something, another dishtowel probably and was wiping himself off. His fluids and hers were now dripping down her thighs. Oh well, there would be plenty of time to clean up before her husband came home.

His footsteps moved away across the carpet, pausing for an instant at the front door. "You're something else, Betty."

He must have read her name off an envelope.

"Liz, you can call me Liz." She said.

II

As she and her husband had been trying for monthsto have a baby, it was no surprise when two weeks later she found herself pregnant, to be confirmed a month later by a test kit, morning sickness, and butterfly marks on her cheeks.

The only question was whether it was her husband's baby or the rapist's.

Not wanting her husband to know what had happened that afternoon, she had cleaned up carefully, taken a shower, and then inspected herself in the mirror. Finding tiny bite marks on her breasts that might or might not turn into hickeys the next day, she made sure that when her husband came home that evening she was wearing only the skimpiest of clothing.

Once undressed, she insisted that he bite her breasts and suck her tits before she would let him inside her. She tried to get him to go down on her but, as always, he was reluctant. At any rate, any evidence of the intruder's presence was covered up by the next day.

Life went by without further incident, until several weeks into her second trimester, when one of the other tenants in their building had the bright idea of holding a building-wide party.

The idea was a success, the majority of the party goers motivated as Liz's husband seemed to be by the desire to see more of some other tenant or tenants whom they had only glimpsed coming and going from the building.

The object of her husband's attentions appeared to be a skinny blond that one of the other tenants had said made her living as a model. I'd like to see him get off on her tits, Liz thought.

Abandoned by her husband, she roamed the fringes of the party hoping she might bump into someone who would hold the same fascination for her. Perhaps her pregnancy was keeping the men away

The man who stood next to her by the counter separating the living room from the kitchen, dressed in white shirt and chinos, was tall and athletic, handsome as a male model. He even smelled good.

Still, she was the one who had to start the conversation— which surprised her, she might be pregnant, but she was easily the best-looking woman there. When he replied, finally, she knew why he'd remained so quiet.

He was the rapist, had to be. She recognized the voice, and, now she came to think of it, she recognized the masculine aroma that emanated from him.

"What apartment are you in?" she asked, trying to act as if she didn't really have any hidden motivation such as calling the police the minute she got back to her apartment.

"Oh, I don't live in the building."

They were both quiet for several minutes while the party went on noisily around them. How on earth had he gotten into the building? Downstairs in the front lobby were security cameras, double locks on the doors, and a doorman on duty, at least during daylight hours.

"It's noisy in here, isn't it?" the man said.

She nodded her agreement.

"Would you like to go some place quiet?"

Again she nodded. He would probably try to take her to his building a few doors up or down the street. Once she had the address, she could work on getting the apartment number.

But instead of leading her down the stairs to the street, they took the elevator up to the top floor and then walked up the stairs to the roof.

"The door up here is locked, isn't it?" The door to the roof had been locked the one time she tried it. But the door was not locked now and in a moment they were outside in the fresh air, the lights of the city stretching off into the distance below.

"It's beautiful," she said, somewhat hesitantly. She did not like heights. Looking out to her left she saw that the next building, a duplicate of hers, was only a few feet away.

"You could jump the gap, I guess," she said.

"Or you could use that board over there to build a bridge." Which explained how he must have got into her building. Getting into her apartment would have been even easier; a credit card could do it unless she or her husband remembered to lock the dead bolt, which they seldom did.

"You're a very beautiful woman," he said.

"I'm a very pregnant woman," she replied. And a very horny one, she thought; the second trimester she'd learned was always like that—three months of ecstasy, given the right stimulus, that is. "You can eat me if you want," she offered.

He owed her one, if he was the rapist that is. Either way, she couldn't lose on the arrangement. Let her husband flirt all he wanted with the skinny model

"I'll be glad to." He led her around the back of the elevator housing, kneeled on the tar, slipped her panties down as he had months earlier and went to work. He was as skilled with his tongue as with his other member and it didn't take long for her to climax. He could come inside her now if he wanted and she very much wanted him to.

The door slammed on the other side of the elevator where they'd stepped out on the roof a moment before. They could hear voices. "I'm sorry," she said as she bent down and slipped her panties back up her other leg, "I guess you'll have to wait."

"That's O.K. I owed you one."

He was the rapist! All at once she forgave him. He had given her several excellent orgasms after all. "You can come to my apartment tomorrow at three if you like. Can you make it?" He nodded that he could.

They traded places with the other couple—the man from apartment 19, the woman from 27—and walked back to the stairway. Everyone seemed to be having a good time that night and she wondered idly how her husband was doing with his skinny model. The answer, judging by the fierceness with which he attacked her when they were in bed that night, was that he'd struck out.

III

The rapist, his name was Frank he'd told her, was not in her apartment the next day at three when she returned. A half hour later, she'd just about decided he was not coming after all, when he appeared in the doorway credit card in hand.

"Sorry I'm late. Your next door neighbor was fussing about in the hallway when I got here so I had to go back upstairs."

Her next-door neighbor, an elderly woman, was indeed very nosy and she thanked him for his discretion.

"Oh, and you really ought to lock that deadbolt." She laughed.

"Shall we try the kitchen again or would you prefer the bedroom?"

They tried both the kitchen and the living room. For the time being, she decided, the bedroom would be strictly reserved for her husband. They also tried both the sitting and the from-the-rear positions.

"We won't be able to use the sitting position much longer. Pity, your breasts are so incredibly beautiful, now. Tell me," he asked, after she'd place his hand on her belly to feel the kicking infant. "Is this my child or his?"

"I don't know," she replied truthfully.

They agreed to meet again the following week, this time in a motel, to avoid all possibility of discovery. The motel was expensive, but she did not want to be seen going into his apartment building or have him be seen going into hers. The charges began to add up though.

When she realized that once a week might not be often enough for him or for her, she would walk to the park, he would pick her up there in his automobile and she would either give him a blow job or he would reward her with his agile tongue. Alas, with her protruding belly, there wasn't room for much else.

Of course, her husband still needed to be satisfied, but during her second trimester this was no problem and a twice-daily workout seemed to be just what the doctor ordered.

Occasionally, she would look rather hungrily at a well-hung delivery boy, and once, at a very attractive (and married) man on the third floor of her building, but she always refrained.

In the last months of her pregnancy, she wasn't able to see Frank very often, even a walk in the park could be difficult, but he still arranged to sneak into see her. With her husband also displaying a keen interest in her breasts, she hoped there would be enough milk for their child when he or she finally arrived.

Then abruptly, the baby was there and every waking hour seemed to be filled with things for the two of them to do. One day she realized she hadn't seen her lover in more than a month and had to ask herself whether she really wanted to again.

Seeing him would mean hiring a sitter. But she'd been planning to hire one anyway in order to go back to her part time job. Her husband had no objection. The girl she chose finally was an 18-year old named Katie, not too much in the breast department but with red hair, freckles, and a skin like fresh cream. Katie proved to be very good with Robert, Jr. for she was relaxed from the beginning, even though Liz was still quite nervous.

"I've taken care of all my younger brothers. Babies aren't fragile, they don't break, and you needn't worry about the bairn when he's with me."

Liz asked her once if she was planning to have bairns herself. "After a bit, perhaps. I'm saving my money and Conrad is too."

"Do you and Conrad, you know?" Liz asked her later on after a few weeks had gone by and they were close friends. Katie had recoiled in horror. "Not till we're married. If you start doing that sort of thing, you can't stop, I've been told. Conrad had me touch his thing once, through the pants. He liked it, but I knew I couldn't do it again. It wouldn't be right."

Liz wanted to hug the girl. Indeed she wanted to do more than that, but contented herself with a kiss on Katie's cheek, after which she went out the door, though she did not go shopping as she'd told Katie, but to the motel, where she did a great many things with Frank that Katie and Conrad probably hadn't even thought of doing.

She was sitting up in bed with her second husband, as she'd grown to think of him, when Frank asked her about the girl. "She's very pretty."

"Her name's Katie and she's a virgin." Liz told him, "Would you like to screw her?"

"Very much so. If you wouldn't mind?"

"Not at all, there's a thing or two I'd like to do with her myself. Now here's my plan."

IV

When Katie stepped into Liz's living room the next morning, she recoiled with horror. Liz was tied to a chair, naked, while a man stood above her holding an upraised butcher knife. He'd covered his head and face with a pair of nylon hose so that his features were all distorted.

"Help me," Liz cried.

Katie started to head from the room to get help but the man's hand was already on her shoulder. "Not so fast."

"Help me," Liz repeated. "He's going to rape me."

"Not necessarily, depends on your friend."

"What? What do you want?" Katie stammered.

"I want to see your tits."

"No," she replied weakly. No one had ever seen her small breasts apart from her mother and her mirror.

"He's got a knife," Liz said.

"Unbutton your blouse and I won't hurt her or you."

She turned; perhaps she could still get away. But as quickly, he turned her around again. "Will you unbutton your blouse or will I just rip the buttons off."

The lace blouse was a good one and had cost her many hours of babysitting. Slowly, unwillingly, she unfastened each of its buttons.

"Now your bra," he said as he pulled the ends of the blouse roughly from her skirt.

"Please," Liz said as if it were she who were being threatened.

Katie reached behind her back and again complied with what the man demanded. She was doubly ashamed. Not only because she stood naked in front of a man, but because her own beasts seemed so tiny compared with Liz's large beautiful ones.

The man whistled. "Just beautiful." He looked down intently at her breasts and then slowly up into Katie's eyes, "I so much want to caress them.

"But I won't," he added hastily when he saw her reaction. "Now, I want you to kneel before your friend."

Katie turned and knelt slowly facing Liz, the man's hands pressing on her shoulders. She wanted to look away having never been this close to another woman's private parts before, but he held her so she could not move.

"Now, you will either do what I say or I will rape this woman."

"No," Liz cried.

"What do you want me to do?" Katie smiled up at Liz so that she needn't look at what was wet and glistening before her.

"Kiss her. No, don't get up," he added when Katie started to rise. He held her back and urged her forward.

She thought, he wants me to kiss Liz's. . ."

"I want you to kiss her pussy."

"Please or he'll rape me."

"I'll rape her," the man said and Katie saw that he had unzipped his fly and was now brandishing what to her was an enormous penis.

She took a deep breath, bent forward, and gave what was meant to be a quick kiss on Liz's swollen vaginal lips. But when she tried to move away, she found her head held firmly in place.

Liz had bent down was whispering in her ear. It was Liz's hands not Frank's that held Katie's head but she wasn't to know that. "Use your tongue," Liz said.

Katie flicked out her tongue. Once when she and Conrad her fiancé were kissing he'd stuck his tongue inside her mouth. She'd stuck out her own tongue immediately before she realized how wrong that was. Now her tongue was licking the inner edges of Liz's pussy, then thrusting inside, her mouth tasting then swallowing the overflowing juices.

She felt dizzy and her arms reached out automatically for support, encircling Liz's waist. For an instant, Katie's hand reached up and caressed one of Liz's ample breasts before as quickly she tore it away.

Liz grinned upward at Frank acknowledging the gesture. Her thighs gripped Katie's head firmly as her legs went around the girl's back. She, too, had no intention of letting go until she'd had her pleasure.

Katie had begun to lick and suck in earnest not knowing that the juices she swallowed were a mixture of Frank's and her friend's, nor that her own juices had begun to spill around the edges of her cunt.

She felt fingers now toying with her nipples, a man's arms around her back. Strangely, their presence only made her feel warmer and more comfortable, less afraid.

She barely reacted when her panties were pulled down her thighs, then over one ankle. The man's finger probed at her vagina. Conrad had tried to put his finger there once, but of course she wouldn't let him, not until they were married.

It wasn't a finger. As wet or wetter than she'd ever been before, Frank's penis slid easily into her vagina, only requiring a little force as the last of her hymen tore away.

He began to move his cock in and out slowly, his hands all the while massaging her breasts and stroking her nipples. A wave of ecstasy began to spread slowly though her body at the same time as with sudden convulsions Liz began to buck in the chair pulling Katie up and down and Frank in and out with each movement.

The pressure on Katie's ears and head suddenly eased up as Liz released her hold. But Frank had not let go. He thrust harder and harder now, turning her and moving her across the carpet with each thrust. She gave a little cry at the same time that she could feel his liquid surging up inside her.

A moment later, she was standing up, Liz's arms around her from behind. Liz caressing her breasts, kissing her hair, saying over and over, "It's all right."

The next day Katie would be shown a picture. It showed her standing, Liz's hand on her bare breast, Liz holding up Katie's skirt in front so that Katie was naked from the waist down, her cunt hairs glistening wet, a dribble of cum on her thigh along with several spots of blood.

V

Katie had stayed with the baby that day, though Liz had offered to let her go home if she needed to. "I don't really need to go out today." But Katie had insisted. It was her job and besides taking care of the baby would allow her to keep her mind off what had just happened, on what, if anything, she could tell Conrad.

She had not planned on going back to Liz's house the following morning, but Liz had called and begged her to come. "You were the one who saved me. You can't possibly be embarrassed. You only did the things you did to help me. I will always be grateful."

When she had got to Liz's apartment, Liz had hugged her and given her a long, lingering kiss, one that had ended only when Katie broke them apart.

"This isn't right," she said, "two women like this."

'But yesterday we were so intimate. You saved me."

Katie shook her head. She and Liz had been intimate, true; but it was wrong all wrong.

It was then that Liz showed her the photograph. "What if I were to show Conrad this picture?" Liz asked.

She had led Katie to the bedroom then, propped herself up on the pillows, with her knees spread apart, revealing that there was nothing under her robe, nothing that could come between their mutual enjoyment.

Katie set to work, at first unwillingly, and then as Liz began to caress her breast and finger her clitoris, enthusiastically. When Liz had climaxed, finally, she insisted that Katie take one of her swollen breasts in her mouth and lie beside her.

Katie was surprised to find that Liz's breast was filled with milk, though she shouldn't have been, and she sucked greedily, ashamed she might be stealing the milk from the baby. "Don't worry, he gets plenty." Liz said.

Every fiber in Katie's body wanted Liz to move her finger still resting so lightly on Katie's clitoris, to bring her to the ecstasy she'd felt the day before. She heard a footstep, felt rather than saw Liz looking up, heard her say, "She's ready."

Katie was not really surprised to see the tall handsome man standing there, the mask no longer on his face.

While Liz stood up from the bed and put on her robe, the man lifted Katie up and placed her head on the pillow Liz had just vacated. Then the man lay where Katie had lain and began to suck gently on Katie's breast. She never wanted him to stop, wanted to have a baby so that her breasts too would be large and filled with milk. Then his mouth was down where her mouth had been on Liz, his tongue licking the edges of her vulva, sucking on her clitoris, bringing her almost, but again not quite to her climax.

He pushed up on his elbows then and stared down at her. She reached up quickly and kissed him. He took her hand and guided it to his stiff, erect member. It felt so long, so soft, so beautiful. "Put me inside you," he whispered. Conrad has asked her once just to touch it through his pants; she'd refused, told him they had to wait till they were married. Now, she fumbled a little fitting Frank's penis to her opening; he was so large, the opening so small, would he ever get inside?

But he did and she came at once with a brief cry. He was not through with her though. He lay still just holding her for a moment and she felt her vagina beginning to pulse of its own accord, gripping and releasing him, gripping and releasing. Then he was moving back and forth, back and forth, slowly as if they had all the time in the world, and she was thrusting her hips up from the bed, eager to get him all inside her, reluctant to let him withdraw.

Once, slowly, deliberately, he withdrew his penis almost all the way out of her. "No," she cried.

"No what?"

"No, I want you to fuck me, fuck me." And he did sliding his penis in and out in long strokes.

She lost all control over her body, could not believe the words coming out of her mouth, dug her nails into his back. Now, she was on top. He was biting her breasts, was thrusting in and out. She screamed as he seemed to empty a bucket of his cum inside her.

Then, they were side by side on the bed, his hand on one breast, her hand on his penis.

They were lying that way a half hour later, when Liz came back into the room, still wearing only her robe.

"I see you've almost restored him," she said, referring to the somewhat enlarged penis that Katie now held in her hand.

"Do you know what to do now?"

Katie shook her head.

"I'll teach you. I'll teach you everything." Liz lay down beside Frank on the opposite side of the bed from Katie, her head on the level with his waist and indicated that Katie should slide down and join her.

"Do what I do," Liz said and proceeded to use her tongue to lick upwards from the foot of Frank's shaft to the elongating tip. She stopped and supervised as Katie duplicated the movement. Then the two of them set to work in earnest, licking and nibbling. "Pretend it's an ice-cream cone," Liz said and Katie began to lick the tip tasting the last remaining drops of her own fluids mixed with Frank's. And then, because she couldn't restrain herself any longer, swallowing as much of his member as she could, till, no longer asleep, Frank exploded once more. His cum ran down the edges of her mouth, she choked, and then his cum was everywhere, in her hair, covering her face, dripping onto her breasts.

She saw a flash of light and sat up, Frank rising to sit beside her

Liz straddled the foot of the bed, the camera that had been used the day before in her hand. "You two make a perfect couple. Have you given any thought to marrying her?" Liz asked.

"Marrying her?" Frank repeated. It was clear that this struck him as a rather off-the-wall idea. Katie on the other hand, looked up at him as if she couldn't imagine anything more delightful.

Liz crawled over and whispered in Frank's ear. "If the two of you were married, I could visit you anytime I wanted; it would not be as if you were single, a threat to my husband, or someone the neighbors would talk about."

This being a very good plan—Frank had already experienced some difficulty getting in and out of Liz's apartment without being seen by the very nosy older woman across the way, he adopted it instantly. He proposed to Katie, was accepted, and before Conrad might have thought to offer an objection, the two were married and Katie ensconced in Frank's apartment.

Liz visited them often, spending quality time with each of them, individually as well as together, to everyone's satisfaction. Katie had taken up Liz's offer to let her be the one to break the news to Conrad, and Liz, on the pretext of consoling him, had done just that and more besides.

Liz's husband took a shine to Katie and during the final weeks of Liz's second pregnancy had suggested that perhaps he and Katie might be intimate. Unlike the hapless Conrad, she reacted indignantly, telling Liz's husband in no uncertain terms that she was and always had been a one-man woman.

Jay

The two apartment buildings around the corner that mar this area are quite different in nature. Though the lobby is quite run down, the apartments in Liz's building, large and high-ceiling, should and do attract professionals like Liz's husband. The apartments next door are far smaller; the landlord promises to repaint the interior walls and replace the missing light bulbs in the hallways but never actually follows through. If like Cecile, you're an underpaid spinster librarian, then you rent what you can afford and try to make the best of it.

Cecile's Diary

I am writing to describe an almost unfortunate incident that happened to me the other day because I do not always bother to lock as well as close my front door when I come in from the outside.

Shortly after I returned from the grocery store this Friday—I was lucky enough to have the day off and to be able to use the time to catch up on all my undone household chores—I was in the kitchen, putting away the groceries, when the door that I thought I had locked and bolted, burst open, and two young men, somewhere between 17 and 19, stood just inside my living room.

I thought I recognized them as living in one or the other of the many apartments in my complex, but there are so many apartments with harried single-mothers trying to cope with their over-hormoned teenagers that I could not be sure.

"Hi," I said, "I think you're in the wrong apartment."

"No," said the darker and larger of the two, "I think we're in the right place." The dark-haired boy was not very tall, perhaps 5'8" or 5'9" at most, but he had a broad thick chest as if he lifted weights. He had very dark hair, which he wore in the duck-back style of the fifties. A dark gray-black wool jacket with leather patches bore the name of his school and the patches on his sleeve told me he had made the team in both wrestling and football. His lips were set in an ugly, almost permanent smirk that just begged to be slapped away. Had there not been such a great difference in height and build between the two of us, I might have slapped him then and there. I should have slapped him many times that afternoon but was afraid of the punishment he would extract in return. This one is the problem, I thought.

"My name is Charlie," he said. I said nothing. His slight blond male companion was "Bill." Bill looked ordinary, even likable if he had not been standing uninvited in my living room.

Still, I wondered why they were there. I did not have long to wait.

"Take off your sweater," Charlie said advancing into the kitchen.

"I will not."

"Then we'll cut it off." He took a large clasp knife from his jacket pocket and opened the blade. My gray woolen sweater-skirt combination is one of my more expensive outfits. I'm not sure now why I wore it to the grocery store.

"No Charlie," his friend intervened, "You said there wouldn't be any violence." Bill smiled at me, and I relaxed, thinking, thank God one of them is sane. Then Bill looked at me and his eyes were as wild and strange as those of his friend: "Please Miss, pull up your sweater so we can see.

"Please Miss." I did what they asked; I did not think I had any choice; somehow, the thought that I could scream, yell, resist, did not even occur to me.

With my arms pinned up over my head by the sweater, I was in no position to resist anything. In moments, they had unhooked my bra and were pushing me stumbling across my own front room.

Charlie's hands were all over my body—I thought it was Charlie, I was blinded, of course, by the thick wool of my sweater—cupping my breasts, probing my thighs, even as I twisted and tried to break away, doing silly things with his fingers along my back. He, they, stopped poking at me finally, but only because they—Charlie and Bill, were by now both sucking on my nipples, my two breasts undergoing such frenzied handling as only a mother of twins or triplets might comprehend.

The sucking styles of the two boys were completely different. Charlie—I judged it was Charlie by the smell, he seemed the least likely to bathe regularly—alternated a frenzied biting motion with an almost infant-like passiveness in which he gave himself up to my breast. Bill was more exploratory, licking me gently, kissing the swell of my breast as well as the nipple and leaving me completely unresisting.

"Mfff," I said quietly, "I can't breathe." They lifted the front of my sweater, then pulled it over the top of my head so that my arms were free. "Be careful," I said. I can't believe that I was still thinking about the expense of replacing the sweater.

I had Bill to thank for my partial release. Charlie was completely engrossed in my nipple and gave little or no indication that he would ever let go. Once Bill was satisfied that I was able to breathe, he returned to his explorations and, when the two of them pulled free, finally, we were all three satiated (four, if you count my two breasts as individuals).

We sat quietly for a while, me on the couch, they kneeling before me on the carpet. I will confess now that at that moment, I no longer though of escape but had given myself up to ecstasy.

Only after several minutes had passed did I remember that I was bare-breasted, that there were teeth marks all over my breasts, one of them at least, and that my nipples were still swollen and protruding as if begging the two boys to begin their sucking and pawing all over again.

They did, several times, and once or twice with my assistance as I held up a drooping head to my bosom. Do not ask the condition of my panties, they were soaking wet.

Charlie stood up first. "I'm hungry," he said and looked toward the kitchen. Bill continued to look at me soulfully, eye-to-eye, until I looked away embarrassed. "I've got to go to the bathroom," I said quietly. At least, I thought I said it quietly, but Charlie, who by now was in the kitchen with his head in the refrigerator, heard and hollered to Bill, "Follow her and see that she doesn't try to get away."

I had no intention of getting away, but they couldn't have known this.

Bill stood outside the bathroom door, like a guard watching over a convict. My bathroom only communicates with the outside world via a ceiling fan, so he didn't have much reason to worry about my escaping. I used the time though to think about escape, and I left the tap water running to mask any embarrassing sounds.

When I came out of the bathroom—I wish now that I had thought to take a fresh pair of panties in with me—it was really obvious how small my apartment is. The one and only bathroom opens off the bedroom, so there we all were, Bill and me and, just a few feet away, the bed.

I smiled. He smiled. It's hard to make conversation when all you're wearing is a skirt and the man you're facing has just dined extensively on your nipples. I knew if he wanted to nibble again, I would not have the power or the desire to resist.

I looked up at the ceiling and all around at the corners of the room, but inevitably my eyes were drawn back to Bill and to the bed. His blue eyes stared back unblinking. I wondered what he was thinking and tried to think about it myself.

"Would you lift up your skirt?" he asked politely.

"What?" I had heard what Bill said, of course, but was trying to stall for time.

"Would you lift up your skirt?" he repeated every bit as politely. "I'd like to see, you know, between your legs."

My nipples, which it seemed to me were already as hard as rocks, stiffened and stood erect as penises. I don't know what I said; I must have murmured something. But the next moment Bill was kneeling in front of me—I was by now sitting on the bed, murmuring, cooing, "please."

"I'm not sure this is a good idea," I began.

"My friend," he began, "My friend would want to force you. I just want to look."

I could hear the friend, Charlie, still moving about in the kitchen. What was he doing there? cooking a meal? I would be all right, I thought, as long as I could keep the two boys separate.

"You just want to look at me?" I questioned. I was very aware of my bare breasts only inches from his lips.

"Stand up please," he said. I don't know why I obeyed, maybe because he asked me so politely, but I stood up. "Now, lift your dress," he asked again. My hands totally out of control, my arms belonging to someone else, I slowly lifted my skirt above my thighs.

He had grabbed a stapler off my desk. "I'll staple your skirt so it stays up," he said.

"No." All I could think of was that my gray crepe was a good if not a terribly expensive dress and I couldn't let him put holes in it. "I'll pin it up," I said. I searched desperately through my dresser drawer until I found the pins.

Now, I stood before him, the hem of my dress pinned up above my waist, while he sat on the bed and looked at me. I could feel the lips of my vagina tingle and hoped he would not notice how damp and receptive I was. Had I shaved? Was body hair showing below my panties? It did not matter. With one swift motion, he had pulled my panties down below my hips. When I resisted, far too late, he grabbed my hands, thrust me down on the bed and began to suck eagerly on one of my swollen nipples.

I sat up abruptly, but he continued to suck as gently as he had the first time when he and Charlie played with me together on the couch. His hand slid slowly up my thigh, I resisted a little, but the strength in my wrist was no match for the strength in his arm and soon his fingers were probing at my clitoris and my dampness had turned into a flood.

We could both hear Charlie moving about in the next room. What Bill was doing to me with his fingers was absolute bliss and I prayed that Charlie would stay away just a little longer. I had passed from passive to active participant in my deflowering, had pulled Bill's head against my breast, stroked his fine blond hair, and was crooning his name over and over. What else did I say, what else did I dream of doing with this young boy half my age?

His other hand lifted my weak hand from his wrist and placed it inside his pants. Slowly, I extracted his swollen member and then pulling myself up and onto his lap, I pushed him inside of me. He came immediately still sucking at my breast.

My thighs were soaked with his cum. "I'm sorry I was so quick," he said; he kissed me lightly on my lips and touched my breast and I came almost immediately though not to the extent a deeper more satisfying penetration would have achieved.

When I looked up, Bill had disappeared inside the bathroom. For a few moments, he fussed about at the sink with the door open, cleaning his member on my bath towel. When he returned, he looked at me for an instant, our eyes making only a single brief contact, and then he left the bedroom heading for the kitchen.

Well, I thought, giggling inanely, now it's Charlie's turn. Quickly, I unpinned my dress and smoothed my skirt down over my thighs. I did not have time to retrieve my panties before Charlie was in the room.

A smear of peanut butter and breadcrumbs was at the corner of his mouth. He had fixed himself a teen-age meal, indeed.

"I hear you gave Bill a good time," he said, that infuriating smirk again taking over his full-lipped mouth. Strangely, I no longer hated that smile; instead I thought, as his mother must have, many times, how handsome he would be without it.

The top two buttons on Charlie's shirt were undone and he proceeded then to unbutton all of them, one at a time, as he if were some kind of male stripper. He was very handsome; the weight lifting had given him the physique of a somewhat older and larger male and I looked away quickly, almost done in by the thought of his scent and how it would feel to have him inside me.

Common sense intervened, thankfully. I had been sitting on the bed while he was undressing and the belated idea came to me that it was the bed as much as my bare breasts that was giving him ideas. I decided to walk away from the bed quickly even though it might and did result in my bare breasts bouncing as I walked.

He followed me as I was trying to slip past him between the bed and the wall and gripped my right breast firmly in his left hand, his right hand holding my head back for an unwanted kiss. Had he persisted, I probably would have ceased resisting. As it was, I opened my mouth to his and pressed back with equal fervor.

But Charlie did not have the courage that Bill had. Oh Charlie could turn me black and blue, pulling on my nipple, twisting my hair, pinching and probing like I was some enormous doll. But he was unwilling or unable to press forward with what we both wanted.

The more his reluctance, the more the words spilled from his mouth. Awful gross things, about his wanting to put his penis in my mouth, about the taste of his cum, and so forth. I wanted him to do everything he talked about but he would not or could not put his words into actions.

Had he had just held me the way a man should hold a woman, lifted my dress as Bill had, I would have coupled with him eagerly, clamped him inside me and held him there as long as he wanted to stay. But in the end, he came against me, unsatisfactorily for both of us, one hand cupped on my buttock, the other hard on my back forcing my bare breasts and distended nipples against his own bare chest.

As I expected, he left me almost the minute he had obtained his own satisfaction, left me and did not once look back.

I could hear them talking in the living room. I could hear Bill say, "No, don't take that, she's a nice lady." When I looked through the crack in the bedroom door, I saw them standing by my front door. Charlie was holding a small soapstone statue I'd purchased while on vacation in Canada. Slowly, and very reluctantly, he put it back down on top of my television.

Then, they'd opened the front door and stepped out of my apartment. I giggled, thought of hollering, "Come back you guys, I'm ready, I'm ready," but fortunately still had a small measure of common sense. As it was, after double-locking my front door—no more leaving anything to chance—I fell back into my bedroom and used my fingers to finish what those boys had unwittingly started.

Just Before We Say Goodbye

Strictly speaking, this last tale doesn't belong in our collection. It concerns my mainly useless attorney son. He doesn't live on this block and I include his story only because for the longest while I didn't think he had a story in him.

Jay

Mrs. Marston

Mrs. Marston had snipped a page out of the February issue of Self magazine and pasted it side by side in the frame with the photographs of her daughter and her husband. The photo depicted a slim, long-legged model with small breasts who posed, head thrown back, aboard a sailboat in what looked to be the Greek Islands.

"Your cousin?" I asked.

"Me," she said. I stared at her.

Mrs. Marston is an ample-bosomed woman of middling height. Her calves are firm and trim, but long-legged? Small-busted?

She may or may not have guessed what I was thinking, for she said, "Not me, now, Mr. Fine, me after I come off my diet."

Impossible. You may shrink from a D cup to a C, Mrs. Marston but, thank the Lord, you will never be as flat chested as the woman in that photograph. What I said aloud, was, "I can see the effects of the diet already, Mrs. Marston. It seems to me, you are looking better every day."

She beamed. Apparently, I'd said exactly the right thing.

You will notice I call Mrs. Marston by her last name, not Alice or Kathy as I might address one of the other secretaries. Something about Mrs. Marston almost impels formality. Still in her thirties — she married young, apparently — she projects the image of someone a good deal older. Perhaps it is the severe tailored clothing she habitually wears, only occasionally relieved by a bright scarf or a cream-colored lace vest. I'm sure her clothes are designed to conceal her bust but, thankfully, nothing can conceal that imposing structure.

She came to work once in one of those baggy sweaters that so hide the figure that one might as well have a man for a secretary. Not so with Mrs. Marston. Her sweater merely emphasized the size and swell of her breasts and I'd had to spend most of my day behind my desk to conceal my erection.

Many times, I came close to asking her to wear that sweater again. But this is an era of political correctness, and our Mrs. Marston is more demure and proper than most. Besides, every one of her sentences seems to begin either with "my husband," or "my daughter." She's a very married, very formal lady, and, I might add, much too good a secretary to risk losing.

Still, there was one occasion, I think it was the second year Mrs. Marston worked for Kimble, Kimble and Fine — I'm Fine by the way, how are you? Not much of a joke, but I thought I'd tell it before you did — midway through summer and she'd come to work in a sleeveless white linen blouse with a cross-over top, the sort of blouse where a man can sometimes play peek-a-boo if he looks down at just the correct angle. I didn't try to play peek-a-boo with Mrs. Marston, of course; I was sure she'd be wearing a solid foundation garment that would spoil the entire effect. This was why the sight of her bare breast, just before quitting time, was so unexpected.

She was bent over, exchanging her high-heeled shoes for the more sensible pair she wears outside the office when one enormous boob fell forward out of its halter and stared at me. Beyond my wildest fantasies, a huge pink melon, firm as that of a young girl in her late teens, whose stem was an enormous purple-tipped nipple that just begged to be sucked.

I looked away at once, not wanting to embarrass Mrs. Marston. Still, I'm sure she knew I'd seen her breast for like the legendary baggy sweater, she never wore that particular blouse to work again.

Mrs. Marston's diet went on for some time, though the effects were not immediately noticeable. She'd always had a relatively slender waist, considering how much she had available on top; her ankles were slim and tapered, and she had thighs and calves that most men would consider perfect to begin with.

What I did notice was that she seemed to be terribly unhappy. She made frequent personal telephone calls, something she'd never done before. From what I could overhear, she seemed to be calling the construction sites where her husband worked, only to be told he wasn't there or was off at lunch.

One day, I found her crying. I looked around, embarrassed, afraid someone else, less forgiving, might have seen her. Fortunately, it was midway through the lunch period and she and I were the only ones in the office.

"Do I look unattractive?" she said to me.

I took pains to assure her she was quite attractive, pointing out that she had a pretty face and soft feminine hair.

"But do I look like that?" she asked, pointing to the woman in the photo on her desk.

I stammered something about it not really mattering, that different people could be attractive in different ways.

She fumbled for a moment with the buttons at the front of her blouse, a nervous gesture, I assumed, and then, gradually, the soft whiteness of her breasts became apparent. Button by button, she was taking off her clothes.

I panicked. Almost one o'clock, the rest of the staff would be coming back from lunch soon. Looking around quickly to confirm we were still alone, I reached out a hand to stop her.

Too late, she had already unfastened the snaps of her bra. Reaching down, she picked up one great breast as if it were nothing more than a melon in a display case and held it out to me.

"Am I attractive?" she repeated.

What could I say to her? Not a good idea. I'm the boss; you're an employee. People will be coming back from lunch at any moment. We could be sued. I'm a married man; my wife counts on me to be faithful.

But I said none of those things. Instead, I took her nipple between my lips and sucked as if I'd not had a feeding for thirty years. Indeed I hadn't, not from a tit as full and ripe as hers, not from a long thick purple-tipped nipple.

"I want to touch him," she said.

"Who," I asked, coming up for air.

"Charlie." And when she saw the puzzlement on my face, added, "that's what I call him. I've seen him jutting out, ready to go so many times when you thought I wasn't looking."

She unzipped my fly then and bent over my penis, sucking hungrily at my cock almost before it was free from my pants. I continued to stroke her huge ripe Casabas.

"Your breasts are so beautiful," I said.

She looked up at me and smiled, her pink tongue darting out for a moment to lick a drop of saliva from her lips. Giving my penis a flick with one long tapered fingernail, she said, "And where would Charlie like to put himself, next?"

She looked up at the wall clock, then, and, I swear, calculated how much time we had till the others returned from lunch.

"Not enough," she said, and still talking to my penis, added, "I'll tell you what we can do instead."

She took off her blouse and tossed her bra, a great gray ugly thing that could have been used for a team flag across the back of her chair. Her enormous bosoms bore a light pink flush, reddened where the bra had imprisoned them, pure white elsewhere with only a few light veins showing through her translucent skin.

Dark brown aureoles the size of Frisbees capped her melons; in each Frisbee's center, a huge firm purple nipple beckoned, still distended from the earlier sucking I had given it. I reached for her breasts again, but she grabbed my wrists and held them, transferring my hands upward to her shoulders.

"I know where we're going to put Charlie." She guided my penis between her great breasts and began to slide him up and down in the narrow space between. I leaned forward and sank my lips into her perfumed hair, squeezing the outsides of her enormous breasts, reaching with my fingers for her nipples. She grasped my testicles and squeezed back in return. In an instant, I lost every bit of self-control; my body convulsed, Charlie shot back and forth between her globes, trying to escape, and then I came, thick and hot. I could feel the wetness cascading down across her breasts and a patch of thick white cum suddenly appeared across one dark brown aureole.

"God, I'm sorry," I apologized. Trapped by her breasts, my cum had shot upward, even spilling across her chin and cheeks. "I'll get a handkerchief."

She shook her head, no, and licked the cum from her mouth and chin, smacking her lips. Using her hand, she gathered more of my cum from her neck and shoulders, lapping it up as if it had been the only meal she'd longed for in her weeks of dieting.

"You don't need to," I began again, apologetically.

"I want to," she said, and leaning down again over my penis, she tickled my thighs with her long full nipples as she sucked the last remaining drops from Charlie.

After we were dressed, I apologized a third time. "I'm afraid you never got a chance to have the same pleasure, I did."

Mrs. Marston smiled at me; despite our workout, she was every bit, as fresh, as cherubic as she had appeared that morning. "But I will get my pleasure, Mr. Fine," she said, "this afternoon after work, when we go to a motel."

For the second time that day, I panicked. I can't go to a motel with you, I thought, my wife is expecting me.

But I didn't have a chance to voice my thoughts aloud. The secretary we'd seen a moment earlier chose that moment to exit from the copy room.

A client arrived next for his one o'clock appointment. Mrs. Marston brought me the file and, a moment later, two cups of coffee and some biscuits on a silver tray, dignified, professional, just as she'd always been.

"A fine looking woman," the client said and, as always, I nodded agreement.

The afternoon crept by.

I spoke to another client on the telephone, and spent fifteen minutes closeted with the senior Kimball hearing about his golf game. All the rest of time I was thinking, I can't go to a motel with her, I've got to go home.

My wife Carole is a beautiful, highly talented woman. A healthy near-vegetarian diet and plenty of tennis and golf have kept her looking nearly as slim and pretty as when we first met. She's a little broader in the hips, perhaps, and she's really never had that much of a bust. Certainly, she's never had enough that I would have thought of sliding Charlie back and forth between her bosoms, or of bouncing up and down on a motel bed with a pair of huge round melons cushioning each stroke, and slender purple nipples to be sucked on before and after.

A half hour before quitting time, I picked up the telephone and called my wife. "Darling, I'm afraid I'm going to have to work late this evening."